KT-416-379

The Song From Somewhere Else

The Song From Somewhere Else

A.F. Harrold

Illustrated by Levi Pinfold

BLOOMSBURY

LONDON OXFORD NEW YORK NEW DELHI SYDNEY

Bloomsbury Publishing, London, Oxford, New York, New Delhi and Sydney

First published in Great Britain in November 2016 by Bloomsbury Publishing Plc
50 Bedford Square, London WC1B 3DP

www.bloomsbury.com

BLOOMSBURY is a registered trademark of Bloomsbury Publishing Plc

A CIP catalogue record for this book is available from the British Library

Hardback ISBN 978 1 4088 5336 8
Export ISBN 978 1 4088 7933 7

All papers used by Bloomsbury Publishing are natural, recyclable products made
from wood grown in well managed forests. The manufacturing processes conform
to the environmental regulations of the country of origin

Printed in China by C&C Offset Printing Co Ltd, Shenzhen, Guangdong

1 3 5 7 9 10 8 6 4 2

For Stephen Dumbrill, Richard Ponsford and Mark Sullivan
– for remembering things how they never happened
A.F. HARROLD

For Carly
– thank you
LEVI PINFOLD

CONTENTS

The Stolen Orange

When I went out I stole an orange
I kept it in my pocket
It felt like a warm planet

Everywhere I went smelt of oranges
Whenever I got into an awkward situation
I'd take the orange out and smell it

And immediately on even dead branches I saw
The lovely and fierce orange blossom
That smells so much of joy

When I went out I stole an orange
It was a safeguard against imagining
There was nothing bright or special in this world

Brian Patten
from Collected Love Poems

MONDAY

After tea Frank cycled over to the rec.

'Come straight back,' her dad had said.

In her bag she had a sheaf of posters. They were A4 bits of paper her mum had photocopied at work with a picture of Quintilius Minimus in the middle and the words MISSING CAT at the top. Underneath, in smaller writing, it said: PLEASE CHECK SHEDS AND GARAGES. IF FOUND PHONE ... and it listed several phone numbers.

Leaning her bike against the fence, she walked over to the slide and pulled out the first poster. Using a roll of tape, she stuck it up. It fluttered in the evening wind, so she added some more to be extra certain.

'Look at this. A missing little *puddy tat*.'

She turned and her stomach shrivelled.

'*Fwancethca* lost her liddle *puddy tat*?'

It wasn't a friendly question. The person asking it in that teasing hateful baby talk was Neil Noble. He was a year above her at school and hated her. No, that wasn't quite true, was it? He didn't *hate* her. He was *obsessed* with her. He sought her out, found her in

the playground, stumbled across her at lunchtime, followed her as she walked home from school, and she didn't know why.

'You not talking? Not going to answer?' he teased. 'What's wrong? *Cat* got your tongue?'

He laughed at his sort-of joke.

The two lads who stood just behind him laughed too.

They always followed him round, this pair, Roy and Rob. They never said much, never started things, just listened, watched, were the audience for Noble's show. If he were to vanish one day, they'd be left standing around not knowing what to do. He was the one that really mattered.

'N-n-no,' Frank stuttered.

She hated herself for that.

The boys laughed, their eyes narrow and flashing.

She never stuttered at home. She never stuttered in class. She never stuttered at all, except at times like this.

Noble took hold of the corner of the poster Frank had just taped up and ripped it from the metal pole. He tore it into little pieces.

'Your *dead* cat,' he said, looking off into the air, 'what's it called?'

Frank knew several things at once.

Firstly, if she *didn't* answer he'd poke and prod with more questions. Maybe he'd start making up stupid names, rude names.

Secondly, if she *did* tell him her cat's name he'd laugh, because cats are usually called normal, boring things like Mouse or Douglas, not magnificent and dignified things like Quintilius Minimus.

And thirdly, her heart was pounding fast and faster in her chest and her stomach was trembling. She was afraid. Afraid of him, afraid of what he might do next, but also afraid that he was right, that Quintilius Minimus *was* dead. It was a thought she'd tried not to think, but still …

And then, almost without knowing it, she did the worst thing she could have done. She tried to lie: 'He's called …' And for a moment she couldn't think of a name, not a normal cattish name, and the pause dragged on while the boy raised an eyebrow, stroked his chin and stared into her eyes. And then she looked away and said, 'He's called H-H-Hector.'

'Huh-Huh-Hector,' Noble repeated. 'Huh-huh-how puh-puh-posh is that?' He snorted a vile little laugh out of his nose. 'Oh, Hector! Huh-Huh-Hector!' he called, as if summoning the cat home for tea.

His two goons joined in.

'Let's help little *F*wance*th*ca look for her aristocratic cat. Remember, boys, be polite.'

7

The three of them tiptoed round the rec, looking between the swings and on the roundabout, behind the benches and in the shadows under the slide, calling out the cat's name.

'Hector! Huh-Huh-Hector!'

Frank just stood there watching, feeling an inch tall on the inside.

If she tried to run for her bike and cycle off, they'd only follow her. She wasn't fast and they had long legs.

'Hector! Oh, Hector!'

'Sir Hector!'

'Lord Hector of Devonshire, where are you?'

Eventually they stopped.

Noble came back over to her.

'It seems he's nowhere to be found, I'm afraid. But, then again, a *dead* cat's hardly likely to shout back, is it?'

'Hang on, Neil,' Rob said.

Roy chuckled.

'What?' Noble asked.

'I fink I've found him, look.'

Despite everything, for a second, for a fraction of a second, Frank felt something like hope.

'Remember who they are, remember where you are,' her stomach said, pulling her back to reality.

Rob was lifting something out of the playground's bin. It was a sticky splitting carrier bag, slopping sideways, full of who knew what old rubbish. Flies buzzed round it and something like a nappy fell out of it with a slapping thud on to the ground.

'Oh God, Rob,' Roy said, 'that's gross.'

Rob waved the dripping bag at his friend.

A spray of grey bin juice splashed Roy's T-shirt and he yelped, jumped away, flapping and frowning.

Noble laughed. He seemed to enjoy cruelty inside his gang as much as he enjoyed it outside.

'Go on,' he urged, 'get him. Ha ha.'

But then his attention snapped back to Frank.

'Hang on,' he said, his forehead wrinkling as a thought ran across it. 'Isn't your *brother* called Hector?'

'Um, Frank?' said her stomach awkwardly.

As if she could feel any smaller, or worse, or more unhappy, Frank realised that of course he was. Her little brother was only five and in her panic she'd forgotten him entirely. Her mind had gone blank with silence, and yet *his* name had worked its way out on to her tongue.

She said nothing. Looked at the ground. Felt like crying. Didn't.

'Yeah,' Rob said, 'he's mates with our little Sid. Hector was at his burfday party the uvver week.'

Noble stared at her, his thumbs tucked into his belt. She could feel his eyes on her even as she looked away.

'You know what I reckon?' he said after a moment, and with a cold huffing chuckle. 'I reckon she's been lying to us. I reckon there is no cat called Hector and never was. She made it up. Have you been lying to us, *Fwancethca*? Lying to your *fwiends*?'

Frank said nothing. She had turned to clay.

'Eh? Eh?' the boys goaded.

She felt sick.

'Eh? Eh?' they went on.

'Yes,' she heard herself whisper eventually.

'Bad move,' her stomach muttered.

Neil Noble sniggered, and as he sniggered he leant down and snatched up Frank's bag, which had been on the ground between her feet.

He pulled the roll of posters out and handed them to his friends.

'Here you go, boys. She won't be needing these then, after all.'

They began tearing them into little shreds as Noble twirled the bag around his head on its strap.

'Stop it,' Frank said, finally finding a trickle of courage.

'Bad move, yet again,' said her stomach. 'You're really great at this, aren't you?'

'Ooh,' Noble mimicked, his voice all high and wobbly, quite unlike hers. 'Th*top* it, *th*top it!'

And then he let go of her bag.

They both watched as it soared in slow motion across the sky to land with a thud in the deepest, darkest patch of stinging nettles in the whole park.

He held his hands up and made his eyes big with mock worry.

'Oh no, boy*th*,' he squeaked, 'we'd be*ht* go before she ge*tth* all ang*w*y.'

They laughed and filed out of the rec.

Frank just stood there on the edge of tears, on the edge of a precipice.

She could hear them laughing behind her. But quickly it got quieter and then she couldn't hear them any more.

She wasn't sure how long she'd stood there, but she hadn't cried. Though her eyes had got misty, she hadn't cried. She was getting good at that.

She was looking over at where her bag had landed. She thought about her legs, the shorts she was wearing and the sandals. She could feel a cool breeze tickling her skin. She looked at the dark bed of nettles. She didn't look at the fluttering, curling confetti that the wind was twirling round the rec. She wasn't thinking of Quintilius Minimus. She wasn't really thinking of anything much, except unfairness in general and how much she hated being her.

Then she heard a voice from behind her.

It said her name. 'Francesca?'

'Don't turn around,' her stomach said. 'That way lies trouble.'

She turned around and her heart, which had finally steadied itself, slumped. It was Nicholas Underbridge. He was in her class at school, but he wasn't her friend. He sat at the back by himself. He smelt weird. He was big, not fat, just big, broad, tall. Bigger than anyone else her age. Taller than anyone else in their class, even taller than Miss Short, their teacher. He had this funny flat face like it was painted on the front of a stone. No one liked him. He had fleas, they said. He'd broken a chair once by sitting down too suddenly. She'd laughed at him when that had happened.

And now, on top of everything else, he was here. Here and sort of smiling at her.

'I saw what happened,' Nicholas said slowly. 'Are you OK?'

His voice sounded like there was a low, dull grumbling engine underneath it.

She felt embarrassed being alone in the rec with him. She worried that someone might see. She worried that someone would assume they were friends. She'd never hear the end of it.

'No,' she said. Then, 'I mean, yes. I'm fine. It was just a bit of fun.'

'It didn't look it.'

He stood in front of her and blocked out the sun.

'It was nothing,' she said, shrugging. 'You know what they're like.'

'Hmm.' Underbridge didn't sound convinced. Not by what she was saying.

'Your bag,' he said, walking over to the edge of the nettles.

She followed him and together they stared at where her bag

had landed. It was metres and metres off, dead in the middle of the dangerous plants.

'It's a pretty bag,' he said.

It was just a bag, she thought. She was upset because it was *her* bag, not because it was pretty. She wasn't even sure a bag could be pretty.

'Do you remember,' Nicholas said slowly, balancing each word in his mouth as if he were thinking of them one at a time, 'that trip we went on to that place where they'd built those old houses?'

She did remember. It was an open-air museum. There were a whole bunch of buildings from way back in the past, from mediaeval times. But she also remembered the coach trip. The whole of her year had been squeezed into one coach and although they were like sardines in there, lots of people sitting three to each pair of chairs, she remembered Nicholas Underbridge on the back seat. He was all alone. No one would sit next to him, even though there was space, even though there was normally a scramble for the back seat. No one had wanted to catch his fleas. They'd said things like, 'I'll be sick if I have to smell *him* all the way.' Things like that.

Had *she* said it? She didn't think so. She'd sat with Jess and Amanda and had been happily squeezed into a window seat.

Nicholas was still talking as he looked at her bag. 'There was this one house that had flints stuck in the wall,' he said. 'Do you remember? Most of them were just round stones, white ones, dusty like, but there was this one that had been cracked open. Its heart was on display, smooth and shining and just the deep blue, the heart blue, of your bag.'

Frank looked at him sideways. This was too weird.

She'd never had a conversation with him before. Who had? And now he was saying things like this? It was just plain *weird*. Who talked like that?

And before she could answer, not that she knew what to say, Nicholas was no longer standing beside her. He'd surged forward, lumbering his huge feet through the nettles.

Frank's legs prickled; she felt goosebumps shiver across her skin as she watched. Sure, he was wearing boots like a grownup's (thinking about the size of his feet they probably *were* grownups') but he was also wearing shorts. It was a hot day. But he didn't even say 'Ouch'.

He picked her bag up and held it above his head like a racing car driver lifts the trophy when they've won, but when he turned to face Frank his happy grin fell to the ground.

'Oh,' he said.

'Uh oh,' said Frank's stomach.

There was a movement behind her. The gate to the rec creaked. There were footsteps.

'Thought you might still be here,' her most hated voice said. 'Didn't know you were meeting your *boyfriend* though.'

Why couldn't he just leave her alone? What had she ever done to him? Why couldn't she do something to make him stop?

She didn't turn round.

'I'm not her boyfriend,' Nicholas said, making his way back through the nettles. He waded through the swaying plants like deep water, lifting his big legs high up with each step.

There was laughter like knives being dropped.

'Oh God, ha!' Noble wheezed. 'Even Stinky Underbridge doesn't want to be *your* boyfriend!'

They found this hilarious.

'Leave her alone,' Nicholas said. He was out of the nettles now and handed Frank her bag.

'Thank you,' she muttered as she pulled it over her shoulder.

'What's it to you then, Stinker?' Noble asked, poking a finger in Underbridge's chest.

Nicholas pulled himself up to his full height, like a mountain standing to attention.

'My name is Nick,' he said, grinding the words out.

'*Stinker,*' Noble whispered, leaning in close.

Although Nicholas Underbridge was taller than the older boy, and although he was wider and thicker and uglier, he was also heavier, slower, less like a weasel. Frank worried for him.

'Call me Nick,' he said again. He said it quietly, calmly, but she could hear a tiredness in his voice too.

'*Stinker,*' Noble hissed one more time, waving his hand in front of his face as if wafting away the reek.

Behind him Roy and Rob laughed and made being-sick noises,

held their noses, flapped at the air and made the sign of the 'keep away' cross with their fingers.

Nicholas said nothing. He just stood there watching.

The boys doubled over with laughter and delight at their great cleverness.

Frank couldn't take this any longer. It was as if a microwave oven had been whirring away in her chest and now the bell went and dinner was ready.

She grabbed Nicholas's sleeve, tugged it and said, 'C'mon! Run!'

It was only once they were running that Frank realised she'd gone the *wrong way*. The park had two entrances, one which led to the estate she lived on, and one which didn't. And, because of where the boys had been, and because of the direction Nick had headed in, and because her legs had started running without asking her brain, and because it was the closest, she'd dashed towards the wrong one.

She heard the rattle of the low metal fence round the rec as Noble and his gang jumped over it, and she could hear him swearing at Roy and Rob, and at her.

Just because she'd got out of the park, away from them, didn't mean this was over yet, but she stood there on the pavement, catching her breath, looking at the gap in the hedges through which she'd just come. It was back through that gap and across the park that her home lay. It was a long way to go round, all through twisty back streets. She wasn't even sure she knew the route. She'd always crossed the park before.

'Francesca,' Nick said, standing next to her. 'Are you all right?'

'No, not really,' she said.

'I think they're coming,' he said.

'But …' she said, not knowing how the sentence was going to end.

Nick looked at her from his great height and, with a shy smile, said, 'C'mon. Quick. This way.'

And he was off, running.

He wasn't a fast runner and she found it easy to keep up. They could hear their pursuers behind them. Frank knew from experience though, that they weren't the sort of pursuers who actually wanted to *catch* their prey. It wasn't like on the telly, where the lions or the cheetahs chase the antelope until they get their claws in, get their teeth in, get a grip and pull the poor thing down, down, down to be dinner. Noble wasn't like that; he was the lion that loped alongside the antelope calling it names until the antelope started to cry. Only then would he be happy. It was as if he fed on frustration and tears, like a vicious, nightmare hummingbird.

'You're muddling your metaphors, again,' said her stomach.

Things were being shouted from behind. 'Fwancethca's got a boyfriend,' and 'Look at sweaty Stinker run,' and other things;

they were making animal noises and singing insults she either *did* not or *tried* not to understand.

Her heart was thumping and her lungs were tearing inside her chest. Even though they weren't running fast, her legs felt as though they were catching fire on the insides. There was a sharp ache in her side.

'Here,' said Nicholas, steady beside her, pointing down a road on their right.

They were opposite their school.

She walked this way every day during term time, but didn't ever come up these side streets. They were dark with trees and long shadows, and the houses seemed closer together than where she lived. Everyone parked on the street.

'Just up here,' he said, pointing ahead and to the left.

'What is it?' she wheezed.

'Home,' he said.

Oh God, she thought. If anyone ever knew that she'd gone to Nicholas Underbridge's house, no one would *ever* talk to her again. It was bad enough being 'rescued' by him, bad enough having 'rescued' him, but if he thought this meant they were friends or something, she'd never live it down.

There was a puddle in the playground called The Bridgey Puddle, named after him. Kids would try to push each other in. If you got the water from the puddle on you, if it splashed you or if you fell in it, if you stood in it by accident even, everyone would hold their

nose and wave the smell away. It was toxic. It was like playing It or Tag, but with a worse mark, one it was much harder to get rid of.

The thing about that puddle was that even when it hadn't rained, everyone knew where it was, knew that shallow dip in the tarmac, and even when it was bone dry you still kept clear of it. You just knew.

And now she was running straight to The Bridgey House.

They bundled into the front yard, a scrubby patch of mud and dandelions, just ahead of Noble and his cronies.

Nicholas lifted the knocker on the door and knocked. He rang the bell too.

'I haven't got a key,' he said, looking at Frank apologetically.

Her legs wobbled under her and she touched the wall with a hand to hold herself steady.

The footsteps behind them stopped, were replaced with giggling.

'What's wrong?' teased Noble in his baby voice. 'Little Stinky not allowed a key, is he? Poor Fwancethca's left all out in the cold with her great fat B.O.-ey boyfriend. Oh, boo hoo.'

She felt sick.

'Go away,' she said.

'Go away,' they repeated.

'Leave me alone,' she said.

'Leave me alone,' they repeated.

'Stop it,' she said.

'Thtop it,' they repeated.

They weren't stepping on to the Underbridges' land. They were staying on the pavement and she knew, again from experience, that they would stay there for as long as they liked. 'It's a free country,' they'd say. 'You can stand on pavements,' they'd say. 'They're public footpaths,' they'd say. And they'd say a whole lot of other stuff.

No one was opening the door.

'I don't think Dad's home,' Nicholas said.

And as he said it another voice broke in on the scene.

'All right, Nick,' a man called from across the street. 'I'm back now.'

Frank looked. The man, crossing the road and waving a bottle of milk in his hand, looked like a perfectly normal grownup. He had a leather jacket and thinning hair and glasses.

'You brought some friends home? Do they need feeding? I think there's some of that spag bol left, isn't there?'

In that infuriatingly dumb, stupid, blinkered, hopeless way adults have, he couldn't see what was going on. Noble and his goons had shut up when they'd heard him and were just leaning on the wall, grinning like idiots.

''Scuse me, boys,' Mr Underbridge said as he squeezed past them.

No matter what you say, Frank had found (not that she'd ever said much), adults always come back with 'They're just playing about,' or 'Ignore them and they'll go away,' or 'Boys will be boys,' or just 'Don't be so silly, Frank.'

'Can Francesca come in, Dad?' Nicholas asked.

'Yeah, course she can,' his dad said as he pulled a bunch of keys from his pocket. 'What about your other pals?' He gestured over his shoulder with the milk.

'They're not with us,' Nicholas said slowly. 'They're just going.'

The inside of the house wasn't what Frank had expected.

Nick's school jumpers always had food on them and his shirts weren't always washed as often as everyone else's. He certainly never brushed his hair. And everyone knew he smelt, probably had fleas.

But the house didn't seem to be like that.

For a start the hallway was clean and bright. The walls were white, and big colourful abstract pictures hung on them. More pictures were stacked against the wall as if they were waiting to find homes. There were no carpets, but the floorboards were painted white and made it feel like you were on holiday.

It was calm, quiet. Underneath the clumping of their shoes on the floorboards was a quiet quite unlike any she'd ever heard at home. Her brother would always cry in the middle of a silence, or her dad would turn the radio on in the kitchen and let old, boring pop music fill the house.

The only thing, the only odd thing, she thought, was the smell.

It was something like a forest. It wasn't unpleasant, but it didn't smell like indoors. It smelt cold, wet. Not *damp*, but ancient. It wasn't air freshener and polish like her own home, and it wasn't like Jess's house, which always smelt of new paint and old dog. It was odd. That was all.

Nicholas's dad made them both squash. He offered biscuits.

'I don't think we've met before,' he said. 'What did Nick say your name was?'

'Francesca Patel, Dad. She's in my class at school.'

'Most people call me Frank,' she added.

'Frank? Mmm. Well, make yourself at home. Do you guys want to watch TV or something?'

'No,' she said, eating her biscuit. 'Thanks, but I really ought to get back. I was just out putting some posters up. Mum and Dad'll start to worry if I'm not home soon.'

Her heart sank as she thought about the posters that had

been ripped up and sank further as she remembered Quintilius Minimus. In all the 'excitement' he'd quite slipped her mind. That was dreadful.

'Our cat's missing,' she said. 'That's what the posters were for.'

'I'm sorry to hear that,' Nicholas's dad said. 'I can give you a lift home if you like? Make sure you get home safe. The car's out the front. You live far?'

'Just the other side of the park,' she said, and told him the address.

He seemed friendly. Frank liked him.

He went off to find his car keys.

Nicholas was slowly nibbling the edges of his biscuit. He looked up at her. She'd never noticed how grey his eyes were before. They were like stones, like little sea-washed pebbles.

'Is your mum around?' she asked, for something to say. His dad seemed friendly and she imagined his mum might be too. It was a puzzle as to why their kid had turned out so weird, but sometimes that was the way, wasn't it? Nice people probably had kids who were a bit backward and who got picked on and ignored at school all the time. It was called genetics.

'No,' Nick said. 'She's not here, she's … She doesn't live here.'

'Well done,' said her stomach. 'Perfect question.'

Oh, thought Frank. That was embarrassing. She felt suddenly ashamed she'd not known that. (Something in the back of her mind, something like a whisper, made her think that maybe she *had* known that, had heard it somewhere, in the playground or in class.)

To cover her embarrassment, and because she wasn't really thinking, she said something stupid.

'My mum's not home much either. She works a lot.'

Nick looked at her and blinked slowly.

So did her stomach.

After a moment he said, 'You sure you've got to go? Already?' But he said it softly.

'Yeah. I'd better,' she said. 'They'll be worried.'

He wanted her to stay. It was so obvious. *God,* she thought, *Nicholas Underbridge thinks I'm his friend. What am I going to do? No one must know. I'll die of embarrassment.*

Before they left she used their loo.

As Frank sat there, on the toilet under the stairs, she looked at her feet and pondered the situation. How could she dislodge Nicholas, get him to go away and leave her alone? Could she really do that after he'd helped her out, after he'd stood up for her in the way he did? Well, she had to, before anyone saw, before Jess came home from her holiday. It was as simple as that.

And then, as she sat and thought, she heard the strangest sound.

'Shut up and listen,' her stomach said. 'Lend me your ears.'

It was faint, it was spooky, it was distant, far off, and it was quite beautiful.

It was music of a sort she'd never heard before.

She was suddenly filled with shoals of fish, darting and moving like one great whole, darting and flowing this way and that, darting and flashing, hundreds and hundreds of silver fish all moving as if they shared one brain. That was what she saw as she heard this faint, distant music.

It was like overhearing a conversation between your mum and dad about your birthday presents. One you're not supposed to hear. One you've hidden at the top of the stairs to listen in on, purely by accident.

No piece of music she'd ever heard on the radio or in the background of a TV show had ever made her feel so special, had made her feel so cared for, so *improved*.

'Shhh,' hissed her stomach. 'You're thinking too loud.'

Where was it coming from? It seemed to be all around her, sort of, but in the distance. It was odd.

Maybe Mr Underbridge had turned the radio on; but they were about to go out, so why would he have done that? And besides, she could hear the pair of them moving about in the hall outside the loo.

And then the music stopped.

No, it didn't *stop*; it faded and vanished without actually ending.

It had only been faint, almost too faint to hear, she thought now. It was the sort of thing that, had she read it in a book,

the character in the book would have said, 'Maybe I imagined it.' But she wasn't in a book. And she hadn't imagined it. She was certain.

'I'm certain too,' her stomach said, on her side for once.

The kettle clicked off just as she opened the back door. There were rolls of steam churning under the cupboard where the plates lived. The radio was talking in between songs.

'Where have you been?' her mum said, gathering Frank up in a hug and letting her go almost at once. They both stepped backwards. 'We've been worried sick. Your dad's been out looking for you. He's out there now. He found your bike at the rec, but you weren't anywhere.'

Her bike! She'd completely forgotten about it.

'One of the wheels was bent and we didn't know what had happened to you.'

'It's OK, Mum,' Frank said. 'I just went round a friend's house and I forgot about the time.'

'Friend? What friend?'

'Just a boy in my class.'

'What's his name?'

'Nicholas. Nick,' Frank said.

Her mum frowned.

'I don't think I know him.'

'He's tall,' Frank said.

Her mum thought a moment.

'And wide?' she asked. 'Maybe I have seen him. I didn't know you were friends.'

'Well, we're not really,' Frank said. 'I just met him over at the rec and –'

'I *thought* you were putting up posters for Quin? Your dad said he found –'

'There was an accident,' Frank interrupted, knowing what her dad had found at the rec, confettied all over the tarmac. 'There was this dog and it ran over and tore the posters up. It ripped them out my hand and shook them like mad. Nicholas and me had to run away. That's why we went back to his house. He lives over by the school.'

She felt satisfied by this story. It made perfect sense, fitted together neatly. It was usually easier to give her parents a *sort of* version of the truth. It stopped all their stupid nosey questions. A mad dog was better, was less humiliating, than Neil Noble and his thugs.

'A *dog*? Was there anyone around? The owner, I mean? Did you get bit? Let me see. Are you OK?'

'Yeah, yeah. I'm fine, and it wasn't really *mad* or anything, just didn't like the posters. Probably cos they had a photo of Quintilius Minimus on. You know dogs don't like cats. That's just the way it goes.'

'We should get the police to look into it if you've been attacked. And at a playground too.'

Her mum was taking this too seriously now, thinking too hard and talking more to herself than to Frank, but at least she was distracted from the telling off she'd been giving.

'Yeah, there *was* someone,' Frank said, thinking on her feet. 'But they were a bit back. They were running over to the dog, but we ran off before they got there.'

'What did the dog look like?'

'I don't remember.'

'You must remember. Surely, darling?'

'No, I don't remember,' Frank snapped. 'OK?'

'OK,' her mum said gently, lifting her hands. 'How about a cup of tea? Kettle's just boiled.'

'No, thanks. I don't like tea.'

Frank went through to the lounge.

She stared at the television. It wasn't switched on. She watched herself pulling faces on the screen.

She heard the fridge door shut, and her mum appeared in the doorway, clutching her mug in both hands. 'You should have phoned though,' she said. 'That's all.'

'What about Dad?' Frank asked.

'Oh God!' her mum said. 'I forgot! Can you ring him, dear? Tell him you're home. My phone's on the table there.'

Before Frank could pick it up, it rang.

She didn't recognise the name, but read it out to her mum.

'It's work, darling,' she said. 'I've got to take it.'

She put her tea down and, putting the phone to her ear, began one of the long and baffling conversations that were forever interrupting things.

Frank phoned her dad on the old landline instead.

That night Frank lay in her bed staring at the ceiling. There was a full moon and every time a breeze crept through her open window the curtain would flutter and there'd be a ripple of light above her. It was the reflection from the fishpond in the back garden. It was only on a very rare night that the moon and the pond and a gap in the clouds lined up just right.

She waited in between ripples, trying to predict when the next silvery glimpse would come. She never guessed right. It was always much longer between ripples than she hoped.

Nothing made much sense.

She hated those boys so much, but there was nothing, not one thing, she could do about them. It was a year now, more than that, that they'd been picking on her, and she couldn't remember, had no idea, what had started it. She didn't understand it, didn't understand them. They'd poke and poke and poke with their words, just following her around, and if she ever talked back to them (she *tried* to ignore them, like people said you should) they'd just do that thing they had done outside Nicholas's house, repeat it all back, in baby talk.

There was no way to beat them, no way to escape them.

And they never did it when there were people around. If she was with Jess they would ignore her, but the moment Jess was gone they'd be there, poking and prodding with their questions. Frank had tried to explain it to her, but Jess just didn't get it, didn't understand how horrible it was. 'They're just boys,' she'd said, 'of course they're idiots.'

Their game, she knew, was to wind her up until she snapped, until she shouted at them or hit out at them or burst into a blather of tears, and it had happened more than once. They had just laughed and laughed.

She hated being laughed at.

It made her feel powerless – which, of course, she was. She could change nothing.

Ah! There was a flash of moonlight on the ceiling. It rippled, cool and white.

She felt sick. Even the moonlight wasn't enough to take that away. Thinking about Noble made her sick. Not actually sick, just that pre-sick feeling, as if she *might* throw up. It sat there somewhere between her stomach and her throat, clogging her up.

She was almost crying. It was pathetic.

And then from nowhere she remembered the music. That strange music she'd heard hidden away in the house of Nicholas Underbridge.

And then she thought of Nicholas Underbridge. Of how kind he'd been and how she didn't dare return that kindness. It was OK here, here in the dark, where no one could see inside her head or heart, to admit that she'd *almost, sort of* liked him, but she couldn't ever let anyone know that. He was not someone she could be friends with.

No one was friends with him.

But that music. There was something in it, even in the memory of it, that lifted her spirits, that made her feel light and hollow and almost happy.

It made her feel clean.

It was weird, because she didn't even like music much. She'd given up the recorder because of the noise it made.

But she had to hear more of this, had to find out what it was. All she needed to know was the name, then she could get her mum or dad to buy the CD. Tomorrow she'd go and ask. One quick visit. No one would notice. Most of her class were away on holiday. Jess was off in some posh farmhouse in the south of France. They'd never know she'd been round Nick's house. Twice.

Did she just call him Nick? She'd have to watch out for that.

But, in truth, it was only a little worry, and it didn't stop her falling asleep to sweet, calm dreams for the first time in months and months.

TUESDAY

When Frank woke the next morning there was an echo of something dream-like in her ears. Although she couldn't hear the music of the day before, of Nick's house, it was still with her, still in her somewhere.

She tried humming it, but it was impossible to pin down, impossible to recall exactly. She needed to hear it again, to refresh her memory. That was the only answer.

And then, as these thoughts circled her, she looked at herself and realised that she couldn't remember the last time that she'd woken up happy. The last time before this morning.

During breakfast Frank racked her brains to think of an excuse to go knock on Nicholas's door. Had he been Jess, it would've been natural to run round and rattle the letter box and just say, 'Is Jess in?' And, had *she* been Jess, she'd've run over and knocked on a new door without caring. Jess was like that. (Though perhaps, she thought, *not* Nicholas Underbridge's.)

This boy was a completely different kettle of fish. She couldn't just roll up, unexpected and out of the blue.

But when they'd finished eating, her dad said, 'It's a beautiful day, Frank. Be a waste to spend it indoors. Why don't you go out, get some fresh air? Get on your bike!'

It was clear he'd forgiven her for the previous evening. He'd even unbuckled her back wheel and, although it wobbled a tiny bit and *zwooshed* against the brake pad every time it went round, it worked fine.

'Where will I go?' she asked.

'I don't know,' her dad said. 'Is Jess still away? What about Amanda?'

'No one's around,' she said.

'Well, never mind them,' he said, shrugging. 'When I was your age I'd just buzz up and down the street, doing skids and seeing how fast I could go. I'm sure you'll find something to do. Enjoy the freedom, the fresh air, the sunshine. It won't be the summer holidays forever, you know.'

He always went on about his childhood, like it had been a hundred years ago and all in black and white with nothing to do but kick tin cans in the street. Frank didn't believe much of it. She couldn't actually imagine him being a boy, even though they'd shown her photos. They could've been pictures of any boy, she thought. The boy they *said* was him didn't have his beard, and although that wasn't exactly surprising, the boy being only a boy, it meant he didn't look anything like him.

'OK,' she said, scooting forward on her bike using her tiptoes. 'I might go see Nick.'

'Oh, this new boy. Yeah, your mum mentioned him. Where's he live?'

'Lime Avenue,' she said. 'Over by school.'

'Fine,' he said. 'Don't go further than that though. And make sure you're back in time for lunch. I'm cooking salad. OK?'

That was the sort of weird thing he was always saying, trying to sound funny. Jess would laugh but Frank wished he'd just behave like a normal dad.

'OK,' she said.

39

And so five minutes later she was sat on her bike in the Underbridges' front garden.

At the bottom of the close where she lived there was an opening in the hedges round the park where the path went in. (They called it a park, but it was really just a field between the estates with a football pitch marked out for Saturdays and the playground tucked away over in the far corner.) Her heart whimpered whenever she leant to look round the hedge.

It seemed like Noble spent half his time kicking dust up round the rec. If she saw him before he saw her, she'd turn away, go home or do something else instead.

Today though, this morning at least, he hadn't been there, the coast had been clear, but she'd still cycled as quick as she could out of habit.

She dropped her bike on the little patch of scrubby front garden. She'd come this far, but, unsurprised at herself, she now didn't know how to knock. What would she say? All she wanted to do was to ask Nicholas about the music (she didn't want to hang out with him or anything like that), but that seemed rude. It seemed weird, too, to be there at all.

After standing in front of the door for a minute, hand half-lifted to knock, her stomach half-talking her into picking up her bike and going, she heard whistling behind her.

'All right, kid?' a voice said.

She turned and was face to face with a postman.

He shuffled his bag up on his shoulder and handed her a pile of letters.

'I don't –'

'And there's this,' the postman said before she could protest, pulling from his bag a long brown rectangular parcel.

He balanced it on top of the letters she was holding.

'Cheers,' he said, turning and heading across the road, whistling again.

She stood there.

It seemed the decision had been made for her. Had it just been the letters she could have slipped them through the letter box and been off and away, but this parcel wasn't going to fit through, and she couldn't just leave it on the step. Anything could happen to it.

So she knocked.

There was quite a long silence, during which she began

to think no one was home, but then she heard movement and rattling inside and the door opened.

It was Mr Underbridge.

He stared at her as if they'd never met before. But then he pointed and said, 'Francesca Patel.'

She handed him the post.

'A bit young for a summer job, aren't you?'

'I met the postman as I was passing by,' she said. 'He asked me to put these through your door. But that one didn't fit.' She pointed at the parcel.

Mr Underbridge shook the box and, recognising the rattle, said, 'Brushes. Great.' He began teasing off the sticky tape and then he looked up. 'Do you want to come in? Nick's around somewhere.' He looked over his shoulder and called up the stairs. 'Nick? Your friend's here.'

Eek, Frank thought, *there's that word. The F word. Got to be careful. Don't be too friendly.*

'Come in,' Mr Underbridge said. 'Best wheel your bike round the back first.' He pointed up the side of the house. 'I'll meet you at the back door.'

Frank and Nicholas sat in the kitchen drinking squash and eating biscuits again. Mr Underbridge leant in the doorway, sipping his coffee.

'How's Nick getting on at school?' he was asking her. 'He never tells me anything. You know what kids are like.'

Her stomach laughed quietly.

She was a kid. She had a good idea what *she* was like, but she had no idea what Nick was like. She couldn't remember anything about his life at school. Well, nothing that she could tell his dad. How do you say, 'Your son's not very popular cos he's got fleas and smells weird'? The only thing she could smell now was that pleasant yet strange, faint, earthy, foresty smell that she'd noticed the night before. Maybe that's what he smelt like in the classroom and it was just the weirdness, the oddness of it, at school that made people roll their noses at him. Maybe they mistook the cool stony outdoorsiness of it for unwashed clothes.

'Well,' she said, trying to not catch Nicholas's eye as she spoke, 'everyone knows him. They talk about him a lot.' That wasn't a lie.

'Popular, eh? You don't take after me,' Nick's dad said. 'Couldn't stand it myself, all those tests. I just wanted to get some paper out and get drawing. That was all I cared about. Do you draw, Frank?'

'Dad,' Nicholas said pleadingly. 'Leave her alone. She doesn't need an interrogation.' He turned to Frank. 'He's a painter and thinks everyone should be painters.'

'That's not true.' Mr Underbridge was shaking his head. 'There are lots of jobs in this world and many of them are important, but

I don't want them, that's all. I found out what I was early on. I can't do anything else. But, Nick, if you want to grow up to be the second assistant undermanager in the municipal sewerage works, then so be it. Plumbing's important, very important … where would we be without it? But me? I just wouldn't know where to begin.'

As Mr Underbridge was talking, Frank felt a shiver go up her spine. Somewhere, just at the edge of her hearing, she could hear the music again. She still couldn't tell where it was coming from, and a moment later it was gone and she wasn't even sure she'd heard anything at all. Her spine tingled all the same.

'I do like to draw,' she said. 'I do good treasure maps.'

Mr Underbridge smiled.

'Well, I hope one day one of them leads you to the right place to dig,' he said.

Then he took his leave.

He went down the hall and through the door on the right into what would normally be the lounge.

'That's his studio,' Nicholas said. 'Once he shuts the door he's not to be disturbed. He'll be in there all day now, I reckon.'

'What does he paint?'

'Stuff,' Nicholas said. 'Those are his paintings in the hall there. He sells them to hotels to hang in the bedrooms. Next time you're on holiday, check the signature. You might find yourself face to face with an Underbridge original.'

From where they sat, Frank could see the colourful strange blobby canvases stacked against the white walls. Though she couldn't see them well, she remembered them from the night before. She hadn't known they'd been Nick's dad's paintings, but had liked them. She wasn't sure that she'd want to sleep in a room with them though: they might have been full of light and colour, but there was a sadness in them too, as if a shipwreck was happening somewhere just outside the frame. She wondered if maybe it was to do with Nick's mum being … you know … elsewhere. That was the sort of thing an artist would paint about, wasn't it? Were they divorced? Was she dead? Nick hadn't said.

And then … there was that music again. It was quiet, far off. But definitely there.

'What's that music?' she asked Nick, happy to have the opportunity. For some reason she had been worried about just bringing it up out of the blue. Hearing it last night had been like overhearing a secret.

'What music?' Nick said, slowly.

Frank held up her finger, pointed into the air.

'*That* music,' she said, laughing.

Nicholas put his glass of squash down with a heavy-handed bang.

'I can't hear anything.'

He looked at the table. Rolled his fingertip through a mirrored pool where some squash had spilt. Cleared his throat.

The music *was* faint, she thought. Maybe he *didn't* hear it. Maybe his ears were so far off the ground, him being so tall and broad and heavy, that the sound wasn't reaching them. It was a mean thought, she thought as soon as she'd thought it, but she didn't take it back.

'You must. Listen,' she urged.

If only she could tell where it was coming from. It was lifting her heart to hear it, even to hear a hint of it. She smiled. It seemed to wrap around her like a blanket.

She caught herself smiling.

She tried to hum along, tried to catch a melody, catch up with the melody and *la la la* it for him, but it was tricky. It kept slipping away from her, like a cat that didn't want to be caught.

Oh, she thought suddenly, *poor Quintilius Minimus. Where is he?*

'Oh, *that* music,' Nick said, rubbing a finger in his ear. 'Um.

That's just Dad's music that he works to. He likes to listen to it while he paints.'

'Do you know what it's called? Who it is? Who it's by?'

'No.'

'Can we ask him?'

'No, I told you. We're not allowed in when he's working. Why do you want to know, anyway?'

Frank thought. She didn't know quite how to put it into words. How to say what the music made her feel? How to explain it?

A moment went by.

'Here we go,' said her stomach, as if it knew what was coming next.

'I'm not happy,' she said, surprising herself.

'Those boys?'

Nick looked at her, his grey eyes unmoving, unblinking, not unsad in themselves. He didn't laugh.

'Yeah.'

'How long ... ?' he asked.

'Ages,' she said.

'Yeah,' he said.

'But last night ...' she went on, 'last night I heard that music ... when I was here, just before I went home, and it ... I don't know, it ... helped.'

'Yeah,' he said again, nodding. He looked away. Scratched at the table.

It was strange, she thought, talking to *him* like this. *Him* of all people. It was as if he understood somehow, in a way that Jess never did, in a way her parents never could.

'Let's have some more biscuits,' Nicholas said, breaking the spell. 'And then we'll get some paper, draw some maps. I like maps too.'

Half an hour later the kitchen table was covered with maps. Some were real, some were imagined.

Frank had drawn a map of her house.

Nick had replied with a map that explained a book he'd been reading: a long spine of mountains down the middle, a huge forest and a single mountain far off on the right. *Here be the dragon*, he wrote. His handwriting was surprisingly neat considering the size of his hands.

She drew an island the shape of a skull, where Cutthroat Hake had buried not only his treasure, but also his cabin boy to guard it as a ghost.

And, as they drew, the ghost of that faint, echoing, inspiring music buoyed them up; it was the treasure she buried, the gold the dragon guarded.

With it there around them, they didn't even need to talk. And then the phone rang.

It was a harsh interruption, snapping them out of the daydream they'd fallen into.

Nick lumbered as quickly as he could into the hallway, where the phone sat on a little table.

He lifted the receiver and said the number.

After a moment he said, 'Hang on,' and, holding the handset to his wide chest, lumbered back to the kitchen door.

'It's my gran,' he said. 'She rings every week. There's no way to get rid of her. I have to be good and listen. I'll be ten minutes, tops.' And he pulled the kitchen door shut.

Oh well, Frank thought, and leant back over the map she was colouring in.

It was only after a minute that she realised something odd.

The music wasn't any quieter. It was still quiet, but it wasn't *quieter* than it had been.

She'd assumed it was quiet because Mr Underbridge's studio door was shut, but now another door in between his studio and the kitchen was shut too and the music was no quieter.

She had the strangest feeling, as if she'd learnt something important, but she couldn't tell what it was.

As she sat and thought, she knocked a pen with her elbow.

She watched as it rolled across the table and fell to the floor with a clatter.

Pushing her chair backwards she clambered down on to her knees, and as she knelt there on the cold tiles she saw something that made her go, 'Oh!'

The wall opposite her had a gap at the bottom. There was a good half centimetre or so where it didn't reach the floor. It wasn't the whole wall, just a section about the width of a door.

She could hear the low rumble of Nick talking in the hallway.

She clambered to her feet and went over to the wall.

She hadn't noticed this door before because it was painted the same colour as the rest of the kitchen and had a calendar hung on it. A plastic bag full of other plastic bags dangled from a hook at one side, a hook that, she now saw, was actually a latch.

She touched it. Rested her finger on it. It was cold metal, painted white.

She pushed down and on the other side of the door a catch lifted up.

With an outward puff of cool air, the door opened an inch.

Frank tested the door, pulling and pushing it back and forth without fully opening it. It swung easily on silent hinges. She couldn't decide if it was a secret door or not. She did know, however, that it would be wrong to go through it, at least without asking.

She let the door swing open wider and looked in.

The music was louder, clearer.

There were stairs leading down.

The smell of the house, the foresty smell, was stronger now. The air was cool on her face. She heard birdsong, smelt moss, rivers, evening.

Nick might come back at any minute, she thought. He must have known the music was coming from down here, but he'd lied to her. That meant (her brain ticked through the conclusions) that he didn't want her going down those stairs.

But it was unfair, wasn't it, keeping such beautiful music, such kind and forgiving music, such perfect and clear and mysterious music, to himself?

It wasn't *his* music now though, was it? It was hers. It was in her ears, in her brain, sparking electricity across synapses in ways that made her unable to resist it. She was hooked like a fish.

Knowing it was wrong, knowing she shouldn't, she went through. 'Tut tut,' said her stomach, filling itself with butterflies.

The kitchen door swung shut behind her. Not with a *click*, not locking her in anywhere, but with a *shush* of air and a tiny *clink* of the metal latch against its partner on the door frame. A narrow strip of under-door light lit the top of the stairs.

Frank felt the smooth wall with her hand as she edged down, feeling each step with the toe of her shoe. The stairs went straight down until they reached a little flat landing, where they turned to the side and continued on.

The crystal shimmer of the music, the swooping circle of it, was louder now. Not *loud*, but closer, nearer. She could hear other things in it too. There was a sharp, hurtful noise, like a violin playing at the very highest point it could go. It scratched inside her ears.

She had no doubt that she had to get closer to it (even while her stomach spoke sense and said, 'Back upstairs, quick, before you get us both in trouble.'). The music was its own whispered invitation. An invitation she felt bound to accept.

It wasn't dark down there. As she crept round the corner she saw the cellar was filled with light. Not bright light, not like stepping out into daylight, but an indoors light, a late-night light. It almost flickered and as it did the music crackled, as if it were a recording that was beginning to jump.

She could make out the last few steps before her and tiptoed down them as she glanced around the room.

For a moment it looked like the sort of basement you read about in books or saw in films, full of piled-up boxes, junk, old stuff; but then the cellar changed. It flickered, like a candle, and she saw something else … saw something else *through* it all.

There's another room, she thought, *somewhere else, but also here.* It was brighter, neater, emptier. Light fell in this other room from tall windows. Frank heard the music swell, and she saw something move.

There was a desk on the other side of the room, and something was sat there. It clicked buttons on an oversized keyboard with long, fat fingers.

It was bigger than a man. Bigger than anyone she'd ever seen. Not fat, but overgrown in all directions. It was hairless, or almost. It was a woman, perhaps. Flowing robes like sheets fell from its shoulders, clasped there with round gleaming brooches. It was grey and rocky-looking. The word 'troll' echoed in Frank's head, even though she didn't believe in such things; she was a sensible girl, had never believed in fairy tales and children's stories.

'Bet you're glad you're not a goat, all the same,' said her stomach.

'Yes,' she replied, gruffly.

She saw this troll, sat at its desk, *through* the cellar she'd first seen. The boxes hadn't gone, hadn't vanished, but had become wispy, smoky. Or maybe they'd stayed sharp and crisp and it was th~~~~ ~~~~ther room, the one with the desk and the light, that was smoky. Either way she could see through them like a misty window. It was hard to understand, hard to keep straight in her mind. It was as if two places were trying to exist in the same place at the same time.

Her feet asked if they could back away, tiptoe up the stairs and get out of there before it turned, before the thing at the desk turned round and saw her. But the music kept playing, calmed her heart (which should have been beating madly with fear), touched her hot brow like a cool flannel … held her hand, almost.

And then the troll turned round, and it saw her.

The music stopped dead with a click.

Silence fell harder than Frank had ever heard it fall before. It took the wind out of her.

Two tiny white eyes peered at her from a huge, flat, ugly, grey, stony face. Sharp white pinpricks through the mist.

Frank thought nothing.

The troll stared at her. Blinked.

And then it said something.
A voice like a landslide rumbled words she didn't understand, couldn't understand.

It didn't roar at her, didn't growl.

It didn't seem like a very good troll, not the sort you read about in books: the sort that tears people's arms off and eats their insides. It seemed to be, almost, friendly, the way it looked at her with those little eyes.

It said something else and Frank felt the words vibrate in her stomach.

'I told you,' her stomach said, feeling ever so slightly seasick. (It didn't say what it had told her.)

And then, as Frank watched, as she considered stepping forward, as she contemplated taking a step towards the troll instead of away from it, the whole scene faded. The other room was gone and all Frank was left with was the woody smell, and the faint tingle of the music still curling around the hairs at the back of her neck.

She took a deep breath. Stood up straight.

'Be sensible,' she said.

She didn't believe in trolls. Didn't believe in seeing things, except normal things. Didn't believe in things that disappeared. Nothing had just happened, she told herself. Nothing.

The basement was dark, dim, lit only by the light from a row of cobwebbed windows high up on the far side.

Her heart echoed in the junk-crowded, shadow-cornered room.

Something rubbed against her ankles.

She looked down.

There was nothing there, just a draught maybe fluttering a bit of rag across the floor.

'Frank!' called a voice from upstairs. 'Frank! Where are you?'

God, Frank thought. *It's Nick.*

'This wasn't my idea,' her stomach said.

He was going to be mad, going to be angry. How could she explain what she'd just seen? And how could she explain what she'd just *done*? You didn't sneak round other people's houses exploring cellars on your own. It just wasn't on. He had every right to be angry.

Nick looked at her as she shut the door.

She was more scared now than she'd been down there. In the cellar she'd hardly had time to think, but the climb up the stairs had been endless. Now her heart shook like a cat-rattled bird.

'The toilet,' she said.

'Brilliant lie,' her stomach said. 'Utterly convincing, except –'

'What?' Nick said.

'I was looking for the toilet,' she explained weakly.

'It's in the hall,' Nick said, slowly. 'Or there's one upstairs.'

'I didn't want to disturb you,' Frank replied, pointing at the cellar door. 'I saw the door and thought … I mean, I-I-I …' *Oh no,* she thought, *that flipping stutter.* 'I-I-I was l-l-looking …'

Nick didn't say anything for a moment, and then he said, 'What did you find?'

Frank tried to think. What *had* she seen? Back in the kitchen, with the warm summer light washing the terracotta-tiled floor, what had happened in the cellar no longer seemed real. The back door was open. She could hear birds singing, a ball being kicked against a wall. Off in the distance, traffic humming.

'No toilet,' she said. 'Just boxes and old stuff.'

Nick sighed.

'Yeah, it's a bit of an old junk room,' he said. 'You should be careful. You could get lost down there.'

'But …' she began and stopped.

Nick was smiling. He seemed to have relaxed. He wasn't angry after all.

The music was long gone.

A door opened in the hallway.

'Was that your gran, Nick?' Mr Underbridge called.

'Yeah.'

'How was she? What's new up there?'

Frank looked at cupboard doors while Nick and his dad spoke about family things.

The cupboard doors weren't very interesting.

Nick's dad had paint on his hands, and paintbrushes in them. She thought of how she wore one of her dad's old shirts back-to-front to do art at school to keep her own shirt clean. Mr Underbridge hadn't done that; he just had paint on his shirt, speckles and dribbles and splotches. But maybe it *was* one of his own old ones or maybe he bought a new one for each new painting. Her head spun. She sat down quickly.

'You OK?' he asked.

'Yes, fine,' she said. 'Thank you.'

'Are you going to stay for lunch?'

'No,' she said. 'Dad's making lunch.'

'Something nice?'

'No.'

Mr Underbridge snorted a tiny laugh.

'I'd best be off in a minute,' she said, glancing at the clock.

She went out the back door, which had been open all morning to let the warm, fresh, clear summer air in, and turned. There were a couple of steps down on to the little square patio.

Nick stood huge in the doorway, looming over her.

'We OK?' he asked.

'Yeah, course we are,' she said.

He nodded slowly.

'You gonna come back?' he asked.

'Sure,' she said.

As she picked her bike up from the lawn where she'd dumped it earlier, she noticed a row of windows that ran along the bottom of the wall below the kitchen. Grass was growing in front of them and she could see cobwebs. They weren't clean, but they looked into the cellar. (At least something had been real; she'd seen those windows from both sides now.)

She turned to look up at Nick again, smiling, and as she did she could've sworn something like a shadow slipped out from among those cobwebs and slid into the garden.

But it was just a movement in the corner of her eye, and when she turned to look there was nothing there.

'Let's not come back,' her stomach said.

'Maybe I'll come back tomorrow,' Frank replied.

'Cool,' said Nick.

She pushed at the salad with her fork.

'Did you have a good morning?' her dad asked.

'It was OK,' she said.

'What did you do in the end?'

'Went round Nick's. Did some drawing and stuff.'

'That's nice,' he said, shoving a massive lettuce leaf in his mouth and crunching wetly.

Some people in this world are lettuce people, Frank thought, *and some people simply aren't.*

She pushed the leaves around on her plate until she uncovered a cube of salty cheese, speared it and popped it in her mouth. It wasn't very nice.

She didn't need anyone to tell her that what she'd seen in the cellar (or what she'd thought she'd seen in the cellar) wasn't something to mention at home. Her mum and dad weren't the sort of people who believed in ghosts, trolls or otherworldly things. They got embarrassed shouting for Quintilius Minimus from the back door; that's how ordinary they were.

And although Frank herself didn't know what it was she'd seen, didn't know exactly what it meant, the image stayed sharp in the front of her mind, fluttering around like a newspaper in the wind. It crackled and kept reminding her of itself. It didn't *explain* itself, but it didn't go away, not like a dream does when you've woken up. And that meant, she thought finally, that it *must've* been real … whatever it was.

Her dad's mobile phone buzzed on the side.

He leant back in his chair, picked it up and looked at it.

'I don't know the number,' he said, raising an eyebrow at Frank, which was his way of saying, 'Curiouser and curiouser'.

He held it to his ear and said, 'Hello?'

It continued buzzing.

He lowered it, tapped the screen with his finger, then lifted it again and said 'Hello?' a second time.

'Really?' he said.

'Oh, gosh,' he said.

'What's the address?' he said.

Frank, not being an idiot, grabbed a pen and an envelope from the sideboard and put them in front of him.

He wrote down an address.

'Yes, in about half an hour,' he said and hung up.

'Is it Quintilius Minimus?' Frank asked.

'Yes,' he said. 'Someone's found him.'

They picked Hector up from his friend Sanjit's house.

Frank sat in the front seat with the cat cage on her lap. It was empty, except for an old towel and some scattered biscuits in the bottom. 'He'll probably be hungry,' she'd said.

Hector was strapped into the child seat in the back and was quite happy talking to his reflection in the car window.

Frank's head buzzed. Not only was she ten minutes away from being reunited with the best cat in the world, but the morning's events refused to stop turning and turning inside her. It wasn't just the whole seeing-things-in-the-cellar business, but also the whole being-friends-with-Nicholas-Underbridge thing as well. How had *that* happened? How had she *let it* happen? What would she say when Jess came back from holiday? Did she only like him because of the music that came from the ghost-troll-thing in his cellar? Or did she actually like him as a real friend, an ordinary one? It was perplexing, that's what it was.

But now Quintilius Minimus was almost back, maybe she'd understand better. There was something unbalanced about the world while he was missing, something a bit skew-whiff.

The car drew to a stop outside a white-panelled bungalow in a street of white-panelled bungalows. All the front gardens had matching neat rosebushes in them. Frank had been watching the roads as they'd driven, and although they'd gone a roundabout route to get here, they weren't a terribly long way away from where they lived. A fair way for a cat to walk though.

She followed her dad out on to the pavement, holding the cage in front of her.

'You stay there, Hector,' her dad said. 'Guard the car for us.'

They walked up the path together and Frank pressed the doorbell.

Before the *ding-dong* had stopped echoing in the air, the door opened a crack.

'Mr Patel?' an old voice asked from inside.

Frank could just make out a wisp of white hair, a smudge of painted pink cheek, a dark glint of eye.

'Yes, we're here about the cat,' her dad said.

Frank held the cage up to the door.

'Mr Patel?'

'Yes, that's right,' her dad repeated. 'And this is my daughter, Francesca.' He put a hand on Frank's shoulder. 'It's her cat really.'

'I see. You can never be too careful.'

The door shut.

Frank and her dad looked at each other. He raised an eyebrow. Frank giggled nervously.

There was a noise from inside of metal jingling.

The door opened again, slightly wider.

'He turned up at the weekend,' the old lady said. 'Wouldn't go away. I had to share my sandwich. Tuna, it was. Do you have tuna where you come from? It's a sort of fish. I'm a touch fond of it and so is he. But I can't be sharing sandwiches at my time of life. That's what I said to my Marjory ... that's my daughter –'

'I hate to interrupt,' her dad said, interrupting. 'But is the cat here? Frank's got some homework to be doing and I've left some potatoes on the hob. We've really got to get going.'

'Oh,' the old lady said. She looked slightly shocked.

There was a *miaow* from somewhere further inside the house and Frank's heart sank. She let the cage slump in her arms.

A cat that almost looked a *little* like Quintilius Minimus (if you ignored this one's sleek shiny coat and its bright green eyes) walked up the hall and rubbed its head on the old lady's bandaged ankles.

'Oh dear,' said her dad.

'Yeah,' Frank said.

'Oh, here he is,' said the old lady, shuffling her feet away from the cat's nose. 'All yours and don't worry about the reward. I mean, I've got my pension, I get on fine.'

'I'm afraid that's not our cat.'

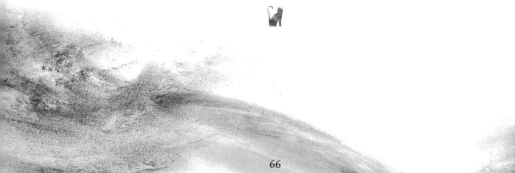

They were silent in the car home.

    'I'm sorry, Frank,' her dad said when he let her in the back door. She put the cage back under the stairs and her dad gave her a hug, whether she wanted it or not.

TUESDAY NIGHT

That night Frank's mum didn't come home. She often had to stay away overnight on business in other towns, but at least, unlike Quintilius Minimus, she always told them beforehand. Frank was used to it.

After her dad had put Hector to bed and then, later, had hustled her off upstairs too, she heard him murmuring softly to her mum on the phone. It was a good noise. It meant *something* was normal.

Now she was finally on her own, without anyone demanding

her attention, she listened to the questions in her head. There were so many of them and they were all speaking at once. Some were still asking her about what had happened in the cellar. About what she had seen. (What *had* she seen?) Some were worried about Quintilius Minimus. Some were wondering how a whole day had managed to go by without it being ruined by Neil Noble. Some asked her if she thought Nick was OK, if she thought he was happy, if she thought he was thinking about her. Some were thinking about that other cat, the one that had turned up at the old lady's house. Was it going to be OK? (Maybe they should have taken it home with them anyway.) How come there were so many missing cats these days?

Underneath it all, her stomach grumbled to itself in words she couldn't quite make out.

It must have been somewhere in amongst all these thoughts, worries and questions that Frank had fallen asleep, because suddenly she woke up.

It was dark. The landing light was off.

She reached out with her foot under the covers as she always did when she woke in the night. There was no heavy, warm, snoring-purring lump down the end.

She got out of bed and crept over to the window. She slipped herself under the curtain and looked out.

She could see stars and she could tell that the moon was out, full or nearly full. It must have been round the other side of the house, because the garden was silvery, except for the nearby bit that was in darkness.

Out of the shadows stepped a cat. Yet another cat!

Or was it Quintilius Minimus?

In the greyness of the night she couldn't tell. Was it him?

As she watched, it moved away, slid through the night, across the lawn, between shrubs, and she was no longer sure it was even a cat. The way it moved was like water, flowing.

She shivered, even though the night was warm.

'Oh,' her stomach said, peering over the edge of the window sill, 'that's not a cat. It's just a shadow that's got nothing casting it.'

Over the fence it went, strange and shapelessly, sniffing the night with no nose, moving with no legs. A shadow-thing. Silent, and gone.

Frank wondered if she was still dreaming.

It had been so strange.

And with that thought, the thought of strangeness, she found she was suddenly thinking about Nick's house. What might be happening there right now? What if she was missing something important? She wanted to see the troll, to hear the music, to know the secret again.

A crazy idea bobbed up in her brain. ('Just go!' it said.) She didn't know where it came from because she didn't recognise it at all. It wasn't the sort of thought she normally thought. ('Just go!' it said again.) It was bold, adventurous, mad. It was the sort of

idea that the people she read about in books might have, not her.
('Just go!' it urged a third time.) It was the sort of thought that
could get her in trouble, and she tried to avoid trouble.

The thought sat there looking at her. After a moment, it said,
'Look, I'm so crazy an idea, aren't I, that you wouldn't think me,
would you, Frank?'

'No,' she said. 'I wouldn't.'

'And yet here I am,' said the idea, holding out its hand for her
to shake.

'Yes,' she said, shaking the idea by the hand. 'Here you are.'

It was a good firm handshake.

'You're probably dreaming,' said the idea. 'That would explain it.'

'Yes, it might,' Frank said, seeing the sense. 'I can imagine dreaming an idea like you.'

'Well, that's settled then,' said the idea, climbing back inside her head.

It's as simple as that, Frank thought: *I'm probably still asleep.*

You're not responsible for your dreams. No one can blame you if you do bad things in your sleep world. It doesn't hurt anyone; it doesn't affect anyone. No one need ever know about it.

In your dreams even your Neil Nobles are defeatable. No one can stop you playing dirty, saying the things you really think, kicking the boys where it really hurts.

Although, all that being said, and all that being true, even in Frank's dreams Noble still won, usually.

Her mind made up, she ducked out from the curtains, back into her room and, in the dark, pulled her dressing gown on over her pyjamas, then tiptoed out on to the landing, down the stairs, through the lounge, into the kitchen and over to the back door.

Beside it was the under-the-stairs cupboard and she pulled a pair of trainers out and slipped them on her feet.

The key hung on the hook and she reached it down, unlocked the door.

She closed it behind her, just pulling it shut, not locking it, leaving the key on the inside.

She lifted her bike from where her dad had told her not to leave it on the patio and walked it out the gate. She thought of when she'd been a little kid, back before Hector was born, thought of all those times she'd declared that she was running away from home, when she'd packed a rucksack and got as far as the dustbins before turning back.

Tonight she wasn't running away and she wouldn't turn back.

She'd never cycled at night before, not in a dream-night nor a real-night. She still pretended she wasn't sure which sort this was.

There were no streetlights across the park, but the tarmac path reflected the moonlight like a winding glass stream with dark gulfs of grass on either side.

She couldn't imagine Neil and his cronies hanging out by the swings at this time of night (the kitchen clock had said it was two), but she cycled fast anyway. Her stomach turned over uncomfortably inside her as she thought of them, as she glanced across at the rec, as they didn't appear.

Out through the hedges she followed the path as it became pavement, bounced down into the road without looking. The night was almost silent, the only noise was the regular *zwoosh* of her wheel rim against the brake pad.

Shadows ran alongside her between the streetlamps, like dolphins racing a boat.

The school playing field was on her left, behind a chain-link fence. She thought of the times she'd had to run round it, the times she'd sat beneath one of the trees at lunchtime trying to read while Noble 'accidentally' kicked a football at her.

Now it was asleep.

She could hear it breathing gently as it dreamt her cycling past.

She turned right, pedalling slower now, cycling up the middle of Nick's road. All the houses were unlit, their curtains drawn, their doors locked. They were asleep too. There were cars parked on either side of the road. They were dreaming metal dreams, winning great races in far-off lands. At intervals, behind the cars and narrowing the pavements, were tall, dark trees, and behind them front gardens and wheelie bins, all fast asleep.

She unhooked her leg and scooted the last few metres with one foot on a pedal, the other just touching the ground. She lifted the bike between two cars and on to the pavement, walked it down the passage at the side of the Underbridges' house, round into the back garden.

She laid it down on the grass, gently, quietly.

For a moment she stood there, wondering what happened

next, almost wondering why she'd come here, and then she knelt down on the grass.

In front of her was the dip down to the cellar windows.

They glowed.

It wasn't reflected moonlight, wasn't the night shining. The glow came from within. There was something happening in there.

She lay on her belly, scooched forward.

With her hand she waved aside cobwebs. Spiders woke suddenly and found themselves in new places, rolled over, assumed they were dreaming too and went back to sleep.

She could see in.

And now she could hear it. Faint through the closed window, but sharp in the night air, there was the whisper of music. Of *the* music.

Oh goodness!

It was new, it was different, it was ancient. It poured into her like fresh orange juice, sharp and cold and full of vitamins. She knew it was doing her good, gulp by gulp, glass by glass. Each cluster of notes, each diving, vanishing melody, each odd change of rhythm wiped clean her soul.

Moving around in the cellar was a great shape. The troll was at the desk, but, as Frank had thought the last time, it wasn't just a desk: it was a computer or an instrument, or both, a keyboard of some sort. There was a screen the great, ugly, flat-faced monster was peering at. It adjusted things with its huge fingers (long as well as wide) and the music shifted, changed, moved about. Frank didn't understand it exactly, but the troll was making it happen, was making the music.

It's a troll composer, she thought, smiling, then wondered why this had seemed odd.

Being a troll, after all, wasn't a *job*. No more than being a human being was a job. It seemed obvious that you'd get trolls who did all sorts of things. It just made sense. There'd be baker trolls and butcher trolls and music-maker trolls. Why not?

The troll leant back in its chair, rubbed at the bridge of its fat-flat grey nose.

Beyond the troll, Frank could see the faint outline of the cellar, of the real junk-filled cellar under Nick's house, but it was like looking at mist, at shadows in the evening, when everything's blue and far off and hard to see. And then she saw Nick.

He was sat on the second to bottom step of the stairs, far over on the other side of the room.

She saw him in sharp focus, for a moment, and then he faded again, became part of the ghost scene, behind and beyond the troll scene.

But she'd seen him and knew what he was doing. He was listening.

'This is a problem,' said the cat.

She was surprised that she wasn't surprised. She hadn't heard the cat approach, but then, of course, that's the whole point of cats.

She rolled on to her side and looked at it.

'Quintilius Minimus,' she said. 'What are you doing here?'

She didn't ask what, later on, seemed the more obvious question: 'How come if you can talk you've never talked before?' or even: 'Where have you been?'

The cat blinked its odd coloured eyes, licked a foot, rubbed a tatty ear and said, 'Someone is going to notice that window is open before long.'

But the window isn't open, Frank thought. She'd wiped away cobwebs but hadn't even touched the glass or the frame. And then she realised that Quintilius Minimus was talking about what was happening in the cellar. The window that let them see into wherever the troll was.

'It's more than a window,' the cat said. Its voice sounded haughty, bored, as if it wanted to be somewhere else, as if it had something better to be doing. 'It's almost a hole. That's another world on the other side. And where there are holes, or almost-holes, there are always interested parties searching.'

'What do you mean?' she asked.

Quintilius Minimus sighed, as if tired of explaining things, then said, 'Holes can let things in. And let things out. Shadows, for example. Little ones. Harmless ones. Easy to catch. Taste of nothing.'

'Uh-huh,' she said.

'But there are other things out there, people maybe, or maybe-people, looking for a place like this: a window they can open even wider. And not all of them have your best interests in mind,' the cat said, looking over its shoulder. 'A secret only lasts so long.'

'I don't understand,' she said. 'What are you talking about?'

The cat said no more. It sat beside her and looked through the cellar window.

'Are you going to come home?' she asked.

The cat didn't answer, and when she next looked at it it was chewing at something dark, something that wriggled like a mouse might, but which wasn't a mouse.

They watched until the light began to fade and the music began to drift away.

The huge troll woman leant forward, tapped at some keys on the keyboard, picked up a mug and took a swig of what might've been tea, what might've been coffee, what might've been something else entirely, and simply vanished.

The cellar was plunged into darkness, the right and proper darkness of a basement at night.

Frank didn't see Nick turn and slowly climb the stairs, wearily heading up into the house, back to his own bed, but she could imagine it.

After sitting and listening and watching all that, would he feel elated, would he feel good about himself, would he be happy, or would he feel something else? Would he be sad now that the music was gone, now it was over? Would he remember what his days at school were like? Would it all come back to him?

And now the music was gone, *she* felt colder. She remembered Neil Noble. And then she imagined being her dad, getting up for a pee in the middle of the night and just peeking round his daughter's door on his way back to bed and finding her room empty.

She looked around and saw that Quintilius Minimus had gone too.

She hadn't noticed him go.

It was like waking from a dream in a strange place.

'Go home,' her stomach said. 'Go home now. This was the wrong thing to do.'

'I know,' she said, even though she wasn't entirely convinced.

She jumped to her feet.

She pulled her bike up and climbed on, tucking her dressing gown under her bum, only now worrying that it might catch in the back wheel.

The air was cold against her skin. This wasn't a dream; this was late at night and she should be at home, should be in bed, should be asleep.

She pedalled without looking back, without wondering

whether Nick had lifted his curtain before he climbed into bed, whether he'd seen her cycling away, whether he'd wondered about that as he went to sleep.

Shadows moved as she passed them by. Curious shadows slid out of gardens and across the road behind her. Watched her go past. Shadows with nothing there to cast them.

WEDNESDAY

After breakfast she knew she was going to go back to Nick's house. She had no choice. Her heart was uneasy with how she'd treated him.

She'd lied to him yesterday when she'd said she'd seen nothing in the cellar. He knew she'd heard the music, so why had she lied about what she'd seen? Because he'd be angry, she'd thought, about her sneaking around his house without asking. But maybe she'd have to face that anger in order to understand what was going on.

Now, after she'd seen him in the basement, seen *him* seeing the same thing *she* saw, she knew she couldn't pretend nothing had happened. It was clearly his secret, but she knew too and it was unfair of her not to let him know that she knew. Wasn't it?

And what about what Quintilius Minimus had said? All that stuff about other worlds and shadows and … It was hard to remember exactly what the cat had said; come the morning it was misty in her mind like a dream, even though she *knew* it had happened. Hadn't it?

Oh! It was all tangling up in knots.

She didn't *want* to go. She didn't want to be friends with him. She didn't, truth be told, want all the weirdness, but … but she *did* want to hear the music and she *did* want him to like her. There was something special about him, about his house.

She didn't have a choice, did she?

She told her dad where she was going and got on her bike.

Frank turned the corner into the park with the usual questions fogging her brain: would *they* be there?

They were.

Neil Noble and not only Rob and Roy, but half a dozen other lads too. They were set up on the grass with a pair of dropped-jumper goalposts, kicking a football back and forth.

For a moment she'd hoped, with no real hope in the hoping,

that the presence of the other boys, boys who'd never been mean to her, some of whom she'd never even seen before, might hold Noble in check.

Her anti-hope instincts, however, were correct.

As she pushed off with one foot and began pedalling down the path as fast as she could, she heard that lisping hateful version of her name roll out over the grass.

'Fwanc*eth*ca!'

And then, with unnatural aim, and a hollow noise like a gymnasium, the ball hurtled out of nowhere and hit her back wheel.

The bike wobbled, skidded, slid out from under her and she went tumbling across the tarmac and on to the dry, dusty summer-worn grass. The bike clattered away from her, pedals banging on the path, a faint *ding* from the unrung bell hanging in the air.

There was laughter, and through the stinging pain she heard her name coming closer.

'Fwanc*eth*ca, Fwanc*eth*ca!'

'Are you all right?'

'Where'd you learn to ride like that? Clown school?'

'You OK?'

'What an idiot!'

There was a crowd of them round her. They kept blocking and unblocking the sun as they moved about. It flickered in her eyes like an interrogation.

She had the impression some people were holding hands out for her, but all she could hear was the laughter, the jeering of Neil and his pals.

'Cut it out, Neil,' one boy said. 'She came a right cropper there. Look at her knee.'

'Don't worry about that. Fwance*th*ca's not afraid of a little blood,' Noble leered. 'Are you?'

Her knee stung. Looking down, she saw it was grazed. Deep red blood pooled dark in the cut and she felt sick and pale and clammy seeing it.

She pushed her way to her feet. There was blood on her hand too.

'You OK?' someone asked, maybe the boy who'd just spoken.

'Of course she's not OK, dumbo,' Noble sneered. 'Look, she's still *breathing*.'

Rob and Roy grunted approval at this.

'Now, come on, Neil, that's not nice.'

Noble turned to the boy he'd been playing football with a minute earlier and pushed him backwards with both hands.

'What's wrong, *Johnny*,' he simpered, batting his eyelashes and nibbling a fingertip between words. 'Is you in love with the little –'

Frank took this opportunity to pull her bike upright and lean on the handlebars. It rolled forward. The back wheel went all the way round. She threw a leg over and scrabbled her feet on to the pedals.

Blood dribbled down her shin. It was warm and dripped on her foot as she pedalled.

Behind her the two boys were scuffling on the grass.

Someone kicked the football at her again, but this time it missed, rolling alongside her for a while until she turned with the path, skirted the rec and zoomed out the park's other entrance.

Frank was breathing heavily and still pedalling fast as she approached Nick's house.

She was afraid Noble and his pals would have finished their squabble in the park and have started following her. Those sorts of things never lasted long when there was tastier prey around. It was just boys showing off, being idiots.

She freewheeled to a stop, her heart slowing, as she saw Mr Underbridge in the street. He was helping a man in brown overalls put packages into the back of a van.

'Morning, Frank,' he said when he saw her.

Then he noticed her pale face, her bleeding knee, her bloody leg.

'Are you OK? What happened?' he asked, coming over and bending down beside her.

'I fell off,' she said, not tearfully, telling all the truth that needed to be told.

'Nick's in the house somewhere,' he said. 'Take your bike round the back and just go in the kitchen. Shout for him. I'll be in in a second.'

He turned to the man, who was straightening one long, flat bubble-wrapped package against the others in the back of the van.

'Bill,' he said. 'There's only a few more in the hallway. You OK getting them out here yourself? I'll be back in a minute.'

Frank walked her bike up the side of the house and round to the back.

As she lay it down on the lawn, she glanced at the cellar windows.

The overgrown grass in front of them looked flattened, a bit. The windows seemed cleaner, or at least less cobwebby.

'What happened to you?' Nick asked, coming out the back door.

'I fell off my bike,' she replied and said no more.

They went into the kitchen. Nick's dad had already got a green first aid box out of a cupboard.

'You'd better wash your knee,' he said.

She ran the hot tap and tore off some kitchen roll.

Once the blood was cleaned away the graze didn't look so big after all. The blood on her hand had been from her knee, not from another cut. She still felt a little sick, but sitting down helped.

Mr Underbridge held her leg firmly as he dabbed it with antiseptic, found a plaster just the right size and shape, and stuck it over the wound. She noticed that his nails were unevenly cut and speckled with multi-coloured paint. He didn't speak as he did it, just got on with the job.

The man with the van, Bill, called for him from the front of the house.

'You'll be OK now, yeah?' he asked. 'I've got to go do some work.'

Frank and Nick sat at the kitchen table. Nick had made some squash and they sipped at their glasses. It was nice to just be quiet for a bit, Frank thought.

'I didn't know if I'd see you today,' Nick said eventually. 'I mean …'

He let the words hang in the air.

Frank had the feeling she'd had when they'd first met at the rec, although she hadn't thought of it in quite this way before, a feeling that he was older than he seemed. He talked, sometimes, like a grownup, and not one of the stupid annoying ones, but like one from a movie, like someone who knew their lines.

The map she'd drawn the day before, the one of the pirate island, was stuck to the front of the fridge with a cat-shaped magnet.

She drank the rest of her squash all in one go. It was cool and refreshing. Ice cubes clinked against the side of the glass, fell against her lips as she dripped the last drops into her mouth. They were numbing, stinging, but she didn't feel sick any more. Even the aching in her knee seemed to be fading away.

She put the glass down.

'I didn't tell you the truth yesterday,' she said, not knowing how else to begin.

Nick didn't say anything.

'About the … the cellar.'

She nodded at the door behind Nick.

'When I went down there, it was … it was because I just sort of *felt* I had to.' This was hard to explain; the words didn't sound true, but what words would work better? She stumbled forward. 'It was weird. I know I should've asked first. I *knew* I should've asked, but I couldn't help myself. I wanted to hear the music better. I had to. It made me listen, made me follow it.' She chuckled nervously, shaking her head and looking away. 'And then, when I was down there I saw something, but I t-t-told you that I *hadn't* seen something. I'm s-s-sorry. I don't know why I lied, but I didn't want you to be … to be mad. And you've been so kind, and I know I shouldn't have gone down there, not without asking you first. I'm sorry, Nick.'

He sat there, staring at her.

His fingers tapped on the table as if they were practising a new nervous little dance for the big show Saturday night.

'How are you feeling?' he asked suddenly, pointing at her knee.

'Better,' she said. 'A bit better, thanks.'

'Do you play Swingball?'

'What?'

'Swingball. Dad set one up in the garden last summer, but it's boring playing by yourself. He doesn't have time usually.'

She followed him out into the sunlight and fresh air.

In the middle of the lawn was a tall metal pole with a tennis ball attached to it by a long bit of cord. It slid round and round on a spiral of metal at the top. She knew this game but hadn't known what it was called. It was exactly the sort of thing Jess didn't like to play.

They took a bat each and started knocking the ball back and forth, the pole glinting in between them.

'What did you see?' he said, after a bit.

'I don't know, not exactly. There was this *thing*, like a troll or an ogre or something … like something from a story or a movie or a comic … and it was making the music. It was huge and ugly and had a computer or a keyboard… and there was moss growing behind its ears and it was dressed in a toga like a Roman or something, and it was making the music, Nick. That beautiful music came from this *monster*. Like beauty and the beast. And then … then it saw me and the music stopped and it … said something. I don't know if it liked me being there, cos it grumbled and rumbled, but I didn't understand.'

Nick laughed, hit the ball hard with a *thwock*.

'Yeah,' he said. 'She's like Dad. She doesn't like to be disturbed when she's working. And you must've surprised her. She doesn't see many strangers.'

A blanket of warm summer snow fell over the garden when Nick spoke, making everything seem friendly again, fresh and

clean and welcoming. Frank felt better for having said what she'd said. Or rather she felt better for having said what she'd said and not having had Nick throw her out or get mad.

'Have you worked out who she is?' he asked.

'No,' she said, knocking the ball back. 'What do you mean, "who she is"? Who *is* she?'

After a moment's hesitation, during which Frank hit the ball and Nick hit it back and Frank hit it again, he said, 'You know I said my mum wasn't here? How it's just me and Dad here?'

'Yeah.'

'Well, that's *sort of* true. But it's also sort of not true. It's complicated and I really reckon you won't believe me. When I say it out loud it just sounds mad. I've never told anyone before. I've not really had anyone *to* tell.'

He stopped talking, hit the ball and watched it spin round on its spring, until Frank knocked it back.

'The troll?' she asked.

'That's my mum,' said Nick.

'Oh,' said Frank.

'Obviously,' her stomach said, rolling its eyes.

She hit the ball again and said nothing.

'There's these other worlds, you see,' he said. 'Other *universes* and it's to do with maths and physics and everything, but sometimes they touch, they bump up against each other. And when they do, sometimes something can get through. That's what I was told.'

'What do you mean?' she asked.

'In the cellar,' he said, nodding towards the windows Frank had lain beside last night. 'Down there's where another world touches this one. It's like when they touch, a window appears and you can see through for a bit … then they move apart a little and it disappears again.'

She thought of Quintilius Minimus. What was it the cat had said last night? Something about other worlds? Something about trouble? About danger? About shadows?

She swung and missed the ball as it sailed towards her, then away, and Nick batted it back for her.

This was odd.

She'd never known a boy whose mum lived in a different world before. If he'd just told her this, without her having seen what she'd seen, without having heard that unearthly, breath-catching music, she wouldn't have believed him. Of course not. She would have laughed awkwardly and tried to get away, but she *had* seen. She had *heard* the music. She knew Nick was telling her the truth.

'Still,' muttered her stomach, not liking what it was hearing, 'maybe you should run, just to be on the safe side.'

'And that's where I came from. That's how I got here,' he said. 'I got lost when I was a baby; I found myself on the wrong side of the window. I *was found* on the wrong side. On *this* side.'

'But,' said Frank, not thinking of enough words to finish the thought.

'It was an accident,' Nick said. 'Dad says I must've just been in the wrong place at the wrong time. The worlds banged together and somehow I popped through. Dad was drawing late one night and then he heard crying and thought it was the television, except he didn't own a television back then. So he went down to the cellar and found me there, wrapped up and wriggling. And the window had shut and vanished before he got there. There was nothing there; he found nothing down there but a fat, confused baby.'

'You.'

'Yep. Me.'

She knocked the ball back and he missed it and she hit it harder as it went past again, sending it zooming down the coiled spring towards the bottom, towards her winning end.

'What did he do?'

'He did what any dad would do. He took me in. He looked after me.'

It was funny, Frank thought, how easy it was to talk about all this stuff now that they were doing something, now they had to concentrate on the ball. They slipped the words in between the batting, and the pole stood between them like a safety curtain.

'But how did you work out that was where you came from? Did he tell you? Did the window open again?' Frank asked.

'I think it was the music,' Nick said. 'It was the music that first took me down there. I was only little, three or four maybe, and didn't know about any of this stuff, but I think I can remember hearing it coming up through the floor. And it was like being called home. Like a good smell that loops in your nose and pulls you along, like you're floating. At least I think that's what it was like. It was a long time ago. It's hard to remember. It's different now. I mean, now it just is what it is. I can't think what it would be like if the music weren't there.'

Frank could hear the faint echo of the music in her own head.

'She was playing the music for *me*,' Nick went on. 'Playing it to say, "It's all right, really." I knew who she was the moment I saw her. I just knew. I'd not had a mother before, and suddenly I did. It was simple. She was beautiful and she smiled at me, but sadly, you know? And now, whenever I'm sad, she plays her music to make me happy again. It's her way of kissing things better. The only way she has now.'

'This window, this other world,' Frank said, fascinated. 'Do you go through? Do you go through to *there*?'

'Is there Turkish Delight on the other side?' added her stomach. 'Are there talking animals? And a wicked witch? He's having you on, Frank. This is all rubbish.'

'Auntie Mimi tried to explain it to me once,' Nick said. When he saw Frank's questioning face, he added, 'She's just a friend of my dad's, not a real aunt or anything. She knows loads about science and stuff. She used to babysit me sometimes when I was little. She's the one who explained it to us, explained about the other worlds. She's the only other person who knows about this, about me. Well, apart from you, now.'

Frank felt herself blush as she batted the ball back. She was one of just four people (and a cat, she guessed) in the whole world who knew this. (But at the same time, she was one of only *two* people who knew about the lucky pine cone Jess kept in the back of her sock drawer. But that secret just didn't seem quite as interesting now.)

Frank remembered how Quintilius Minimus had said people were searching for the window. She held Nick's secret tight to her chest. Super secret.

'Auntie Mimi told us that when the two worlds banged together, a window between them opened for a moment – became a door, you might say – but then it closed again,' Nick said. 'I popped through that first time, but now it's shut. Somehow though, that bang is still echoing, still bouncing. And each time it echoes the window appears. But only sound gets through now, only light. Each bounce or echo is softer than the one before. Eventually, maybe, it'll stop and we won't be able to see the window at all. I don't know. It's to do with energy and stuff I don't really understand. But the fact is I am stuck here and she's stuck there.'

'Oh,' said Frank. That was such a sad thought. She knew how she felt lying in bed on the nights her mum was away for business, how it just added to her loneliness. To imagine her mum being trapped in another world, unable to touch her at all ... And then she thought of something else.

'Oh God! Nick!' she blustered. 'I didn't mean to be rude. I didn't mean anything by it, but I called her a … a … *troll*. I didn't know she was your mum. It's just she's so big and … well … *trollish*-looking. I didn't mean …'

Her stomach said nothing.

But Nick just laughed, hit the ball so it spun round twice before she could even miss it.

'Do you remember those stories you were told as a kid,' he said, seemingly changing the subject. 'Those old stories that had elves and goblins and ogres in? Stories about babies being stolen by fairies? Or those ones where some girl goes for a walk and comes back home only to find a hundred years have passed by?'

She nodded. The stories she hadn't believed in. Stories she'd never thought you were actually supposed to believe. Fairy tales!

'Auntie Mimi said that's what happened to me. And what happened to me's what happened to them. A world bumps against another one hard enough and something pops through … it could be a person from here goes there or a thing from somewhere else ends up here. And if someone from a world where everyone is small gets stuck here, people might think they were a pixie or gnome or something, mightn't they?' Frank nodded. She understood. 'Where I'm from everyone's just a bit bigger than here, that's all. I guess it's the world where trolls and ogres and giants come from, you know. But that's not for definite. It might be people just made the stories up after all. Who knows?'

He laughed again.

'But look at me! I'm massive. I'm the biggest in the school. I've always been biggest in class, haven't I? I take after her, obviously. I'm *clearly* from somewhere else. It makes sense.'

'Are you going to stop growing?' Frank asked.

'I don't know,' he said, shrugging. 'I'm in another world now. Maybe things will be different here.'

She clipped the ball with her bat, badly, and it lost momentum, fell towards the pole, hardly circling it at all.

Nick leant forward, chipped it up, caught it in his hand and began again.

'I'm sorry,' she said.

'No worries,' he said.

'No,' she said. 'Not for *that*.' (She pointed at the ball with her bat.) 'I mean for everything else. I mean for sneaking round your house. For sticking my nose in. For being nosey and for not telling you the truth straight away. For not trusting you.'

'That's OK,' he said. 'How's your knee?'

She'd forgotten about it, but now it began to throb slowly, not hurting, but letting her know it was still there.

'It's OK,' she said. 'Thanks.'

Nick hit the ball again while she was distracted, and it flew off the top where the catch was broken and bounced into some bushes. Frank had lost.

As Nick lumbered off to fetch the ball, she asked, 'How come I can't hear her now?'

He pulled the tennis ball out of the undergrowth by its string.

'I never know when she's going to be there,' he said. 'She's there most days; sometimes she comes in the night. It's not exactly regular. Sometimes she's already playing her music when I come home from school. I like that. It makes the day good when that happens. But it's these bouncing universes, Frank. They bump together on their own timetable. I never know.'

After Nick had rehooked the ball on to the coil they played another couple of games in silence. There was no need to say anything else right then.

The sun was shining and the world smelt summery. There were flowers among the weeds of the garden and bees buzzed in their strangely lazy-busy way from bush to bush. Though heaped white clouds were building away across the estate, the sky above them was high and blue.

At some point the music began again.

'Whatever you do,' her stomach said, slipping its words into the middle of the morning like stinging nettles in a salad, 'don't listen. Don't go closer. Don't get involved. Secrets never end well. Leave the freak and go home. Jess'll be back from holiday soon. Just go wait for her. Let things be as they always were.'

Everything had been going so well – the morning had unfolded so much better than Frank had expected – that these words, coming from inside her, made her feel like being sick.

She felt like she turned grey. Her breakfast bubbled at the bottom of her throat.

The ball zoomed off the top of the Swingball pole again, bouncing into the undergrowth.

'Ah, leave it,' Nick said. 'Let's go downstairs.'

'What?' said Frank, one hand to her chest, swallowing away the bile.

'Quietly,' said Nick. 'Dad mustn't know.'

He led her indoors. The music swirled around them, brushing their ankles like cats might and silencing Frank's stomach.

Nick opened the door to the cellar and gestured for Frank to go first. Her eyes filled with tears as she went past him and down the stairs.

She and Nick sat together at the bottom of the steps, saying nothing.

In the cellar that was a window to another world, they sat and watched Nick's mum, mountainous and grey, mossy-eared and flat-faced, sitting in a room that was a window to *their* world, weaving her music.

Frank brushed her eyes – it wasn't that she was crying, just that they were over-full. Her heart glowed in her chest. A smile played with her mouth, without her having to think about it.

The troll-mother had looked at them, had smiled, and turned back to her instrument, her device, and sent fast clusters of high notes skittering into the air.

'What's her name?' Frank whispered.

'I don't know,' Nick said.

And so they sat, listening …

And eventually the worlds shifted apart, the window faded away and the music moved beyond the limits of Frank's hearing, and the two of them were sat in the dim cellar in friendly silence.

The stony, earthy forest floor smell filled her lungs like lemonade, as harmless stray shadows curled in the corners like mice.

This was turning out to be one strange summer holiday, Frank thought.

It was only when Frank was halfway across the park, past the rec and halfway home, that she remembered that she should've been worried. Fortunately Noble and the other boys had moved on somewhere else, probably home for their own lunches, so she hadn't needed to worry, but it still felt odd having forgotten them for a moment.

'Did you have a good morning?' her dad asked as she put the cutlery out for their lunch.

'Yeah, it was all right,' she said.

She wasn't going to tell him anything, because he wasn't the sort of person who believed in trolls, or in things that weren't quite trolls but were something else. And other worlds? Forget it!

And although she knew he wasn't the sort of parent who'd ring up the child psychologist as soon as she told him she'd seen her troll-friend's troll-mum in a cellar through a window to another world, she did suspect he was the sort who'd go, 'Oh yes, dear?' sarcastically, and that was almost as bad.

Either that or it would set him off on a story of his own: 'When I was your age I had a friend with a door to another world in *his* cellar who used to …' and so on. That was more than she needed.

'We played some swingball,' she said.

'Did you win, dear?' he asked.

'Almost.'

'Well done.'

He skewered a piece of cold potato on his fork and looked at it before putting it in his mouth and chewing thoughtfully.

'I've made some more posters,' he said after he swallowed.

'For Quintilius Minimus?'

'Yes. I thought we could go round and put some up this afternoon. I've finished the work I needed to get done and Hector's over at Maxim's for yet another birthday party, so I'm all yours, kiddo.'

There was no need for him to call her 'kiddo'.

'OK,' she said.

She didn't feel worried about Quintilius Minimus any more, not since she'd seen him last night. He'd said he'd come back soon, hadn't he? (Sort of.) It didn't really matter if they put posters up or not. But her late-night conversation with the not-quite-missing cat was yet another thing she couldn't very well tell her dad about.

They put posters up on lamp posts and trees right round the block.

Frank stood and scuffed her shoes as her dad explained to one of the neighbours from the other side of the close what they were doing.

The old man had run out in the street waving his stick and accused them of being vandals, of spoiling the look of the estate with their hooliganistic postering.

It took her dad ages to smooth the water and to make the old man understand they were doing something good. He pointed at Frank and she pulled a sad face on cue. It helped a little.

It was only when they reached the rec that things went really wrong.

Noble and his goons were back, two of them standing up on the swings while the third threw a tennis ball at them, and because, to her dad, they just looked like three lads larking about, because he didn't know any better, hadn't spent months insomniac with worry, he walked straight through the little gate that separated the rec from the rest of the park as if it didn't matter.

Frank protested as best she could.

'I already came here,' she said, and, 'Shouldn't we stick some up over by the shops?' and, 'I've got a headache – can we go home?'

None of it worked.

As her dad began taping up a poster, Neil Noble jumped down from the swing and swaggered over to them.

'What's that you're doing, Francesca?' he asked politely.

She didn't say anything.

'Our cat's missing,' her dad said. '*Still* missing.'

'Oh no,' Noble replied, 'I'm sorry to hear that. Is there anything we can do?'

He sounded genuinely sad. Frank hated him. She had the worst feeling about what was going to happen next.

Her stomach turned away in fear, covered its eyes.

'Well, boys,' her dad said, 'if you can check your sheds and garages, just make sure he's not stuck inside, that'd be great. You know what

it's like in the summer. Cats find somewhere cool to sleep, out of the way, in someone else's garden, and then your dad shuts the shed up at the end of the day without looking …'

'Easily done, isn't it?' Neil said.

Her dad nodded.

'Well, we'll all be sure to check when we get home, won't we, boys?'

Roy and Rob grunted yesses.

'We'd hate for anything to happen to Francesca's cat. We hate it when friends of ours are sad. It breaks our hearts, really it does.'

Francesca's dad's phone rang inside his jacket.

'Excuse me,' he said, and half-turned away to answer it.

'Hello?' he said.

'What's that?' he said.

'Oh, really?' he said.

'Yes, yes, OK,' he said.

'Yep, give me ten minutes,' he said.

He switched his phone off and slipped it back in his pocket.

'Look, love,' he said to Frank, 'Hector's thrown a tantrum. He's refusing to eat or to stop eating or something, I didn't exactly understand, but

Mrs Harrison's asked me to come get him.'

'I'll go with you,' Frank said.

'No need for that,' he said. 'You should stay with your pals.'

'N-n-no,' she said.

'Don't be silly,' Noble said, putting his arm round her shoulder and squeezing her close. 'Of course you can stay with us. We'll help you look for your cat. We can help put the posters up.' He slid the roll of posters from her dad's jacket pocket.

'That's a good idea,' her dad said.

'N-n-no,' Frank stuttered. She couldn't get the words out. Her mouth refused to work properly.

Why were parents so stupid sometimes?

'No worries,' Noble said, grinning like a poisoner. 'No worries at all.'

'Brilliant,' said her dad. 'I'd best hurry. Have fun, and don't be late for tea.'

And with that he was gone, half jogging away up the path towards their estate.

He looked back once, and the boys waved at him, smiling vulture smiles.

'So,' Noble said as soon as her dad was out of sight. 'Here we are again, then.'

She didn't know how it had happened, or couldn't think how it had happened, but in just ten minutes she'd spilt the beans, blabbed her big mouth, told the truth.

Of course, that wasn't quite right. She *did* know how it had happened, but maybe she wished she didn't. Wished she'd been a better person, a better friend.

But it had been all, 'You been round Stinker's house again?'

And, 'Is Stinker a good snogger? *Mwah, mwah, mwah.*'

And, 'How many times were you sick?'

And, 'No wonder your cat ran away when it heard you were Stinker's girlfriend.'

And on and on.

She couldn't escape. They blocked her exits. They moved with her when she moved, like cats playing with a scared frog. Like crabs scuttling with the tide.

Her knee began to throb.

As she watched the boys, afraid to take her eyes off them, she thought she saw dark shapes flit behind her, like the shadows of animals, circling the rec.

But the shadows didn't feel nearly as dangerous as Noble did. A seesaw tipped in her mind.

'You're such an idiot,' her stomach said. 'I told you to stay in bed this morning.'

The sun went behind a cloud.

All she wanted at that moment was for Nick to turn up.

What she would have given to see his great big shadow cover the rec, to see him loom over Noble and his boys. They'd pretend not to be worried, not to care, but she knew that with Nick around she'd be safe; she just knew it, even though she also knew that it was she who'd had to rescue him the other day, after he'd rescued her bag. But the point was, there'd be two of them: they'd be together.

But he didn't come.

It was all, 'He's so fat he probably *ate* your cat.'

And, 'Stinker's got cat breath!'

And, 'Nah, no way, he's too slow to catch a cat. You ever seen him try to think?'

Noble made the noise of grinding cogs, his features stuttering on his face, with his tongue poking out the side of his mouth and his eyes crossed.

'Don't be so horrible!' Frank shouted, her angriness surprising her from the inside. 'You don't know *anything*! He's not like that!'

As betrayals go, that one didn't go very far. It was hardly handing over state secrets to foreign powers. But still, the moment the words were out of her mouth she knew she could never take them back. She knew Noble would never let them go.

She'd *stood up* for Stinker Underbridge. She'd made her play, shown her hand and picked her side. There was no way back.

Her stomach said something she didn't catch.

Thirty seconds later she was struggling in the arms of Roy and Rob.

'I'll ask you again,' Noble was saying. 'Tell us this *anything* that we don't know. We don't like being ignorant. You don't get anywhere by not knowing stuff. We're not stupid.' He paused for a second. 'Well, except for Roy,' he said. 'He's a bit thick.' He thought for another second before adding, 'And Rob ain't got much going on up there, have you, Rob?'

Rob and Roy chuckled in agreement. It didn't seem to bother them.

'In fact,' Noble went on, 'they're so forgetful, they might just drop you, purely by accident.'

They were holding Frank over the same deep nettle patch that her bag had ended up in.

Her dad was long gone, and Nick was nowhere around. On the far side of the park she thought she'd seen someone walking a dog, but that would do her no good.

Her eyes glittered with fearful tears. Her arms and legs goosebumped in anticipation.

Of course she'd been stung before. She knew how just one little light-as-air brush from a leaf really hurt and itched and buzzed. Her brain played a movie of that all over her arms and legs and face, showed her wading back out, being brushed again and again by the swaying, broken nettle plants.

There weren't enough dock leaves in the world to cope with that, she thought.

And suddenly she was lying in bed as a little girl with sunburn, the sheets all sandpaper and pain where they touched. She remembered moaning all night, in a strange bed, on holiday. The heat of it, the burning pain, all over her. The smell of calamine lotion that didn't stop the itching. The momentary relief as she scratched, sloughing off flakes of skin, only for the itch to grow worse and worse. Turning over in bed was hell. No position brought relief. There was no way out but through and through and through.

Then she was back in the moment, and more scared than she remembered being, ever. Held in the air, the knowledge that at any moment gravity (which she could feel asking for her, which she could hear whispering up from the centre of the Earth) would override Rob and Roy's strength.

Their hands gripped her tight for now.

They'd never really touched her before, never done anything like this. They'd thrown crab apples at her and tripped her up and snatched her lunch or her bag, played piggy-in-the-middle with her shoes, but never this. Something had changed.

Their hot hands were on her bare legs and arms. It was horrible.

Her stomach turned over, heaving, trying desperately to hide behind itself.

'Go on, then,' Noble sneered. 'Tell us what's so special about lovely old Stinker Underbridge, why're you such bosom buddies all of a sudden. What's *he* got that *we* don't?'

'Nothing,' she said, almost whimpering. 'It's nothing.'

'I don't think it's nothing, is it? You know *something*. Go on. Spill. Tell us his big secret, Fwannie.'

The fear filled her upside-down brain and she said things she didn't mean to say, things that she didn't *want* to say but which might get her put down, set down safely if she just gave them *something*, anything … And all she had to hand was the thing that had been buzzing busy and fresh at the front of her brain.

'I s-s-saw his m-m-mum.'

'He ain't got a mum,' Roy said as she squirmed. 'Everyone knows that. It's just him and his dad. That's why he don't never have no clean clothes on.'

'No, no, no,' she said. 'He d-d-does. Sort of. She … she's in the cellar.'

'What?'

'The cellar?'

'What are you talking about? What do you mean *exactly*?' Noble said, as if he were a policeman taking notes and wanting to get everything straight.

'I went down by myself. I w-w-wasn't meant to be there. I s-s-saw her.'

The secret had been so special to her, the sort she'd never had before. It had filled up so much of her, right to the brim of her brain, that it slipped out too easily, like fresh toothpaste spurting from a softly squeezed brand new tube.

'They keep his mum in the cellar?'

They jiggled her, letting her slip and catching her.

The words fell out.

'I s-s-saw her. T-t-troll!'

There was silence for a moment.

Then the boys all roared with laughter.

'Shall we chuck her, Neil?' Roy asked.

'Nah. This is interesting.' He squinted at Frank. 'He told you this, did he?' Again there was a moment's silence before he spoke again. 'You say *you* saw this … ?'

'Y-y-yes.'

She felt herself slipping in the boys' hands. Clammy hands. Dirty hands. Hot hands.

'You're a flipping weird one, you are,' Neil said, spinning round on his heel. He waved his fingers in a spiral movement by the side of his head. 'But I don't reckon you're lying to us. You wouldn't dare. Not again.' He spat on the ground. 'So, *Fwancethca*, how do *we* see her? You've gotta get us in there. I've never seen a real-life, real, live troll and I don't appreciate not seeing things.'

'No,' she said, the will to resist bubbling momentarily.

'All right, boys. Maybe it is time to let our guest go. One … two …'

As he counted Rob and Roy swung her up high over the nettles.

She felt her stomach gasp in the moment of weightlessness at the top of the swing, and her heart fainted with the thought of being let go.

'There's a window!' she heard herself shout.

Noble must have gestured to his goons, because the swinging slowed and then stopped. She was half dropped on to the tarmac, but the boys still kept hold of her.

'Where?' he asked.

'Long little windows,' she panicked, 'at the t-t-top of the cellar. The b-b-back garden.'

She hated herself, and although that wasn't anything very new, she couldn't remember the hate ever making her feel quite this small before. She smelt bad.

'OK, good,' Noble said, brushing dust off her shoulder with a knife-like smile. 'See? That wasn't too hard, was it? We're all friends here, Fwannie. Just friends, having a bit of fun. But,' he went on, lowering his voice and leaning down beside her ear, 'if I find out you've lied to me *again*, your life won't be worth getting up for in the morning. You got me?'

'She's not always th-th-there,' Frank whimpered into the tarmac.

When Frank next looked around she found she was on her own, sat on the bench, by the hedge. The bag of posters was between her feet. Shadows rubbed against her ankles and slid away, out of sight. The memory of the nearness of the nettles pricked all over. But it was over now. For now.

Why hadn't she just lied? All she had needed to do was tell a single simple lie.

THURSDAY

When they'd gone on holiday the year before, they'd stayed in a static caravan on the Isle of Wight. It had been cramped for the four of them, watching the rain pour down the windows, and Frank hadn't much enjoyed it.

There had been one day though, before the holiday was cut short by an urgent phone call that sent her mum hurrying back to the ferry, when the rain had cleared for an hour. Her dad took her and Hector out to the amusement arcade down by the beach.

She could still see the flashing lights, still hear the ringing of bells and buzzers, still smell the grumpy sweaty woman wedged inside the glass booth who refused to look at them as she gave them change for the machines.

Her dad had made her play on an old pinball machine, and she'd been happy to. You pressed buttons at the sides and little white flippers under the glass moved up and down, sending the marble-sized ball bearing whizzing around the sloped playing board, bouncing off the walls and mushrooms and rubber bands and setting off lights and noises: blaring fanfares and blurted sound effects, and the crazy clatter of the scoreboard.

As she'd played, her dad had recounted some story of his youth, how he used to be a king of the pinball machines, how he and his mates would hang around the arcades all summer playing them and chatting up girls. She didn't really listen (it was hard to hear him over the noise of the machines) but it always made him happy to tell these stories and she remembered the faraway look in his eyes, and Hector covering his ears.

She'd never really thought about it before, but now she felt sorry for the ball. It had no choice where to go: it went where it was sent, bounced around from one thing to another with no say in the matter. She felt just like that this morning, as she woke from the tail end of a dream she didn't remember, but which must've had a pinball machine in it.

She lay there in bed feeling like *she'd* been sent one way and another too, without ever once choosing a direction for herself.

It was because of Quintilius Minimus that she'd been at the rec on Monday, because of Neil Noble she'd met Nick and had gone to his house. The following morning the postman had left her with no choice but to knock. What had she decided for herself? Anything?

Frank hadn't slept well. (She was surprised she'd slept at all.) She'd been full of worry about what she'd done, about what those boys would do with what she'd told them. She worried for Nick. What would Noble do to make his life worse now that he knew? She could already hear him singing insults, taking the mickey and upsetting Nick. What if Noble went and looked through the window? What would happen if he saw Nick's mum? What would happen if he *didn't*? Even the memory of the music hadn't soothed her as it had before.

She'd broken everything.

After breakfast she snapped at her little brother for dancing too loudly.

She missed Quintilius Minimus. And then missing him made her think of his visit and that just brought her back to Nick's house. It was all circles.

She lay on her bed and tried to read, but her heart wasn't in it and her eyes kept slipping off the words. She wished she could turn time back. Just a few days would do it. Quintilius Minimus would be at home and she could lock the cat flap and keep him

in forever, and then she would never have been at the rec on
Monday and would never have gone back to Nick's house and
would never have had a secret to let slip at the merest threat of the
stinging nettles.

'Don't be so stupid,' her stomach muttered, cutting through all
the nonsense. 'You know who's really to blame.'

'But …' she said, not having any good comeback to hand.

Her mind was playing tricks: it was Quintilius Minimus's fault
for going missing; it was Nick's fault for saving her bag; it was
Frank's fault for being weak, for being a bad friend.

Her mind was blaming everyone but the one person whose
fault it all really was: Neil Noble. It didn't dare blame him, as if that
would just draw him closer, make him pay her more attention.

'See what I mean?' her stomach said, twisting round.

'But what can I do?' she asked.

Her stomach said nothing: an answer that was filled with a silent,
smug superiority.

Should she phone Nick and apologise? Tell him what she'd done?

But what could she say?

She'd already lied once and apologised. What would he think?
Would he be able to forgive her again?

What sort of a friend had she turned out to be?

She didn't even worry about the word 'friend' any more: that's
what they'd become … until she'd ruined it all.

Poor Nick.

And then the letter box rattled and she found a postcard from Jess.

Apparently it was sunny in the south of France and she'd been bitten by insects and had swum in a river and had eaten some French bread. But she didn't say what all postcards ought to say: 'Wish you were here.'

If only Jess had taken her with them, then, once again, none of this would have happened. And so yet another blameless person was added to Frank's mental list of fault-makers.

Her stomach gurgled to itself, bored.

She went back upstairs and put the postcard on her bedside table.

It was only then that she saw the picture on the front. It was an ugly gargoyle, carved in stone and hung up on some French church, its tongue sticking out and its eyes bulging. It was so ugly, so silly, so ludicrous that it made her smile.

They were put there to keep evil spirits away, she'd read – that and to be drainpipes for the church roof. She felt slightly better for seeing it. Maybe the gargoyle was working, even just a picture of it.

And as she looked she saw that it wasn't as ugly as she'd first thought. Sure, everything was out of proportion, was distorted like in the political cartoons in the newspaper, but there was something likeable about the gargoyle, something mischievous, perhaps.

In an odd way it reminded her of Nick.

They didn't look the same, save for a similar dusky grey

skin tone, but still, there was *something*. She hoped Nick would be able to keep bad luck away too.

And so the morning went on.

Frank was playing Lego with Hector. They had all the pieces tipped out on a blanket in the front room and were searching for bits of just the right size to complete their models. It was raining outside. The day had turned grey to match her mood.

There was a banging at the front door that didn't sound like a postman.

Her dad was upstairs cleaning the bathroom. She could hear his jangly old music playing on the radio. He obviously hadn't heard the door, so Frank carefully set down her half-finished spaceship and answered it.

She was surprised to find Nick looming on the front step, dripping wet. His bike lay on the path and he left it there as he stepped indoors.

'You're soaked,' Frank said, hoping the worry she felt wasn't showing in her voice. 'What are you doing here?'

He was agitated.

'I didn't know where else to go, so I came here. Frank, I think … something's happened.'

He pulled a crumpled envelope out of his pocket.

She shut the door.

'You'd best take your shoes off,' she said. 'Dad's only just hoovered.'

He handed her the envelope and bent down to undo his laces.

She didn't know if she was supposed to open it or not, so she just looked at the front. In thick felt tip it said *Nicholas Underbridge*. That wasn't that surprising, but it meant that the letter hadn't come through the post: there was no stamp and no address on there, just his name. A fat raindrop had blurred the ink in the middle of the *Underbridge*.

'Someone shoved it through the door this morning,' he said. 'Look inside.'

She turned it over and lifted the flap. It didn't look like it had been stuck down at all, just tucked in. She pulled the sheet of paper out and unfolded it.

Her stomach turned over and said, 'Look Frank, he's dripping on the carpet. Tell him to get lost. Tell him to take his letter with him.'

Written there, in the same ugly felt tip writing, was an internet address, a URL, and glued to the sheet of paper, made up from cut-out pieces of newspaper, was the single sentence: *we're watching you, freek*. It looked like a ransom note from an old TV show.

'What's there?' Frank said, pointing at the URL.

'We don't have the internet,' Nick said. 'I dunno.'

'You don't want to look,' said Frank's stomach. 'Go have a lie down, maybe. Pull the curtains. Go back to bed.'

At the back of the house, behind the dining room, her mum

had a little office. She didn't use it much because she was usually away working, but sometimes, especially at the weekend, when she needed to catch up on something or deal with what she'd just been told in one of her dinner-interrupting phone calls, she'd hide herself away in there and grumble.

Frank led Nick in, waving at little Hector in a friendly, smiley way as they passed through the front room, and switched on the power. The computer whirred and the monitor hummed into life.

She carefully typed the address into the browser.

When the page loaded a video began playing.

The footage was shaky, obviously shot on a phone.

On the screen was a film shot at the back of Nick's house. It was almost dark, late evening perhaps or early morning. The camera was tiptoeing up to the long low windows of the cellar, and there, coming into view, was Nick's mum. It wasn't clear (it wasn't really obvious unless you knew what you were seeing) but there, in that basement room, something large was moving, something person-shaped, something not exactly human.

A hand came into shot and began to tug at the bottom of the window. It shifted and lifted up a few centimetres.

Someone behind the camera muttered something wordless and a second hand slapped at the first.

The window fell shut with a small thud.

The camera whizzed round, showed Neil Noble's face for a fraction of a second before he covered the lens with his hand, saying, 'Don't film me, you idiot.' Then there was a crackle and the video ended.

Frank sat back in silence and switched the computer off.

They were both, it seemed, too stunned to speak.

She heard Nick's stomach rumble, but hers said nothing.

Eventually Nick broke the silence.

He looked paler than ever.

'They'd never really noticed me before,' he said. 'Not really. Not especially. Never cared enough to have a go, I guess. No challenge. But now … well, now I've become a … an irritation, haven't I? I know they've been bullying you,' (Frank flinched at the B word,) 'and now they've moved on to me. Because I helped. Their sort hate people who help, Frank. Which is why you *have to* help. They must've come back last night looking to make trouble and instead they found …'

As he trailed off, Frank said, 'I hate them. Nick, I hate them so much.'

'What if the papers find out?' Nick said. 'What if Dad reads it in the paper? Imagine the headline: MONSTERS IN OUR MIDST. He'll kill me. No one's meant to know. If it gets out I'll lose –'

He was interrupted by a scream in the front room.

They ran back to the lounge as soon as Hector started bawling.

He had a nosebleed and a long piece of Lego sticking out of one nostril.

He was dripping blood down his T-shirt.

'Dad!' Frank shouted.

For a while she thought they might have to go to hospital to have the flat one-by-sixer removed, but her dad managed to ease it out with a little bit of wiggling and promises of chocolate.

'When I was a boy, I remember once …' he began as he waved the liberated piece of plastic in the air.

Frank stopped listening and trudged upstairs to get Hector a clean top.

She sat on his bed and rootled through his drawers and thought about what she'd just seen. Not the Lego business, but the video.

Her first instinct was to own up and tell Nick that it was her fault.

But her second instinct was to hide under the duvet and never come out again.

If he found out what she'd done, he'd never want to see her again, wouldn't want to be friends any more. He'd be so upset and angry, and rightly so.

Her third instinct, after overhearing the second instinct, said, 'But that would be OK, wouldn't it? You didn't want to be his friend in the first place, did you?'

'But it's not as simple as that,' she replied.

'It rarely is,' said her third instinct, before it shuffled off into the shadows, whistling.

She made her way back downstairs and helped her dad get Hector changed and quietened down with a choc ice.

Her dad was asking Nick about school and about what his dad did and how he'd met Frank and embarrassing things like that.

As far as she could tell, Nick hadn't said anything, or nothing much. He certainly knew that he shouldn't mention her problems with Noble. He understood about private things and about not spilling the beans or blabbing to people who didn't need to know. Frank knew about that stuff too, but she wasn't as good at it as he was.

'Do you want to stay for lunch?' her dad asked. 'I'm making pickled herring and olive pancakes with a maple syrup dressing and crunchy bits from the back of the cupboard.'

'Um,' said Nick.

'Ignore him,' Frank said. 'He's just being silly. He thinks he's funny but he's really not.'

Her dad stuck his tongue out at her.

'We could have beans on toast,' she said.

'With sossygus,' added Hector.

'Sossy-gooses,' her dad corrected.

Frank's life was a battle between shame and embarrassment, and today both sides were winning.

'Yeah, OK,' Nick said. 'If you don't mind?'

'You'd best ring your mother and/or father,' her dad said, making Frank cringe even deeper. Why couldn't he just talk normally? Why'd he have to try to be 'fun'?

Having to avoid Hector's bean-juice-covered fingers and to deal with her dad seemed to take Nick's mind off his other problems for a while though. Or at least if he was still worried, he didn't let it show. Not to Frank.

Not having any better plan, they cycled back to Nick's house.

The rain had been letting up and was more like a fine drizzly mist than a shower. It was enough though to mean no one was in the park; no one was hanging out in the rec as they went past, splashing through puddles.

'He'll have to move, have to go away,' Frank's stomach said as they turned the corner into his street. 'That's what happens when you get famous, and he's going to be dead famous when the world sees his secret. Won't be able to move for paparazzi.'

Frank had no answer to that.

They dumped their bikes in the back garden and went into the kitchen.

Mr Underbridge was there eating cornflakes.

'Just having my lunch,' he said, smiling at them. 'You guys all right?'

'Yeah,' Nick said.

He didn't sound convincing to Frank, but that was because she knew what she knew. To the rest of the world that one word had sounded like the response of any ordinary slightly bored kid.

'Good, good,' his dad said.

He crunched the last mouthful of cornflakes and stood up to put the bowl in the sink.

As he turned the tap to run the hot water there was a ringing sound, distant and chiming like a far-off doorbell.

'It's the doorbell,' he said, sounding slightly surprised. 'It's too late for the postman … I'll be back in a minute.'

Frank and Nick were left alone in the kitchen.

'Squash?' she asked.

She knew where the glasses and the bottles were and thought getting on with things as if it were an ordinary day might help defuse the tension. Nick didn't look like he was going to do anything.

And then she heard it, faint and at the edge of hearing as always, but growing louder, growing sweeter and warmer: *the music.*

In her mind's ear a silvery ball of fish swirled together, never touching, darting past each other as, underneath, in the depths something huge moved, darkly, until the fish burst out of the water, becoming like a flock of starlings, a hundred melodies weaving through the sky in coiling, smoky shapes. The music was complicated, hard to follow, unlike anything she'd heard in this world, but it moved straight through her, filling her heart and lullabying her worry to sleep.

'I'd listen while you can,' her stomach said.

'Yes,' she replied.

She wanted to open the cellar door and go down there, but she got on with making the squash instead.

As she turned the tap to fill the glasses, Nick stood over by the kitchen door watching his dad.

She carried the glasses over to him and said, 'What's going on?'

'Shhh,' he said. Then, 'Thank you,' as he took the cold drink from her. 'It's Auntie Mimi.'

She peered round him into the hall.

Mr Underbridge was stood in the doorway, one hand on the door as if he were about to close it. Beyond him she could just make out the figure of a woman. It was hard to see since the afternoon light cast both of them in silhouette.

'No, no, no,' Mr Underbridge was saying, not raising his voice, but shaking his head.

'Time's up,' the woman was saying. 'It's over now.'

Her voice was soft; it was hard to make out everything she said.

'We both knew this day would come. I'm surprised it has taken this long to be honest.'

'I don't …' Mr Underbridge said. 'I can't …' Then, 'Think of the boy.'

'It was thinking of the boy that got us here today. It was my soft heart, my soft head, that let you talk me into leaving the leechway open in the first place.'

'But –'

'It was *highly* irregular.'

'But –'

'Now the secret's spilt, Paul, it won't be long. It'll be hours, probably. Maybe a day. But people *will* be looking for the leechway. They always are. We've been lucky. And if they get control –'

'Yes, yes,' Nick's dad said, sounding tetchy, cutting the woman off with a wave of his hand. 'I see.'

'I can shut it now,' the woman said. 'The work of a moment. I've got a charge in my case. I'll do it right away and we'll be safe.'

Mr Underbridge said nothing for a moment. The door wavered in his hand.

'No,' he said. 'I can't let you do that.'

'It's easy,' she said. 'Just let me in.'

'No,' he said again. 'No. You can't come in. Don't you need a warrant or something?'

'Paul. Please,' she said. For a moment it sounded like she was pleading with him. Then she said in a firmer, take-charge tone of voice, 'Don't play games. Don't make this hard.'

'A warrant,' he said, and pushed the door closed.

The darkness in the hallway was sudden and blinding.

Nick's dad didn't move.

The doorbell rang again and again and still he didn't open the door.

Frank stood behind an equally immobile Nick.

This was her fault, whatever it was, and she didn't know what to do.

And then, finally, Nick moved. He shifted backwards and Frank got out of his way.

He looked stunned. His grey skin was paler than normal, almost white.

'What is it?' she said, just wanting to say something friendly. She already knew, already thought she knew.

Nick took a long swig of his squash as he shuffled further into the kitchen.

'She wants to shut the window. She wants to shut my mum out,' he said.

'Nick, we need to talk,' his dad said, coming into the kitchen.

Frank shuffled backwards, towards the door.

Although it couldn't be true, it looked as if Mr Underbridge had been crying. His eyes were red and glittering and she thought his cheeks were damp.

'Oh, Frank,' he said, 'you're still here.'

'Yes, sorry,' she said.

'You need to go,' he said. 'I need to talk to Nick. Alone. Sorry.'

'O-O-OK,' she said.

She was happy to leave. The atmosphere had turned sour (she hadn't noticed when the music had gone, but it had). But she also wanted to stay. She wanted to be there for Nick, to be with him in the face of all this ... mess. He *was* her friend and it was her fault, after all, even if no one else knew that.

But his dad, Mr Underbridge, was looking at her, sucking his bottom lip and staring as if he wanted her gone.

She realised she wasn't moving and stepped out on to the back step.

She turned and said, 'Cheerio, Nick,' in a voice that was meant to be light and friendly, but which caught in her throat and just sounded weird.

'Bye, Frank,' Nick said, not quite looking at her.

She went out into the garden and turned to leave, but stopped in front of the cellar windows. The clouds were beginning to blow away overhead; the general greyness was lifting. The world smelt like it had been washed in clean water, but with something like gunpowder in the distance.

A stray shadow slid across the patio, as if it were meant to be underneath a weasel or mouse or something, but wasn't; it slid away from the windows into the undergrowth.

She remembered what Quintilius Minimus had said: 'Harmless. Easy to catch. Taste of nothing.'

A few days ago she'd've run a mile if she'd seen such a thing, or simply assumed she'd imagined it. But now ... so much had changed. She was different now; the world was different now.

She didn't mean to eavesdrop, but she could hear the voices in the kitchen. They thought she'd gone. She didn't move.

'I don't know what to do,' said Mr Underbridge.

'What?' said Nick.

'There's a film, apparently. On the internet. Someone's been here. Been out there. Seen down there.'

Nick said nothing.

'You know what I'm talking about?'

Nick said nothing.

'How did they find out? How? Oh, I don't suppose it matters now. They've had the video taken down, but God knows who's seen it. What do we do? What do we do now? Mimi's gone all official. She's freaking out. She wants to close the window, Nick. She's got a thing that will just shut it off. Seal it up, forever.'

'But what about Mum?'

'I know,' said Mr Underbridge.

'It's not fair,' shouted Nick, and she heard him thud off into the house.

His dad said nothing to that, but she thought she heard a sigh and someone sitting down, shuffling papers.

'Go,' said her stomach. 'Get out of here.'

Frank made her way up the side of the house and out on to the pavement.

She was about to get on her bike when a voice stopped her.

'Excuse me. Young lady?'

In the middle of the road, looking up at the Underbridges' house, was a woman. This must be Auntie Mimi.

She looked normal enough. She was quite old, probably in her forties, with streaks of grey in her tied-back black hair. She wore a dark suit, like Frank's mum's, but more battered. There were scuff marks and paler patches, as if she'd rubbed up against dusty or mucky things and hadn't sent it to the dry cleaner's yet. She pulled off a pair of dark glasses and twiddled them in her hand. In her other hand was a briefcase.

Frank stopped where she was and said nothing.

The woman came over.

'You don't live here, do you?'

'No,' said Frank, slowly.

She could hear the sound of an amusement arcade dinging in the back of her head somewhere. She had the giddy sensation she'd just been ricocheted from one place to another, that she was still just a ball hurtling around the machine to someone else's tune. Where was she going now?

The woman looked at Frank closely, blocking her way and not letting her past. She looked serious.

Frank thought back to how the conversation on the doorstep

had ended. Mr Underbridge had sent her away, this family friend, this woman who'd babysat Nick, this Auntie Mimi, telling her she couldn't come in, not unless she came back with a warrant.

A *warrant*?

Frank thought about that word. She'd heard people say it on television shows. It was what the police needed to have before they could search your house, wasn't it? Was Auntie Mimi a policewoman? It didn't sound like a policewoman's name, Mimi.

'Are you the police?' Frank asked.

The woman laughed briefly.

'In a manner of speaking … no,' she said. She narrowed her eyes. 'What makes you ask?'

'Nick's dad,' Frank said. 'He said you needed to get a warrant.'

Frank was surprised she hadn't stuttered. This woman was making her nervous, slightly, at the very edges. She had eyes that caught hold of yours and looked into them. As much as Frank wanted to look away, as uncomfortable as she felt, she found she couldn't.

'You heard that?'

Frank nodded. She probably hadn't been meant to hear it.

'What's your name?' the woman asked.

'Francesca,' Francesca said. And then, when there was no answer to that, 'Francesca Patel.'

'Patel? A good strong name,' the woman replied. 'I like it. I'm Special Agent Jofolofski, Department of Extra-Existent Affairs.'

She flashed a card in a wallet too quickly for Frank to read anything. 'So, you're a friend of Nicholas?'

Frank said, 'Yes.' This was the first time she'd admitted it out loud. It was an easy thing to say. She didn't know how she'd explain it to Jess or to the rest of her class come September, but at some point that had stopped being important.

'If you want to help him, you should do something for me. Francesca, dear, *you* don't need a warrant to go into the house. They like you. They'll let you in. All you need to do is take a little *thing* into the cellar for me.' She paused, tapped the arm of her dark glasses against her teeth and peered at Frank. 'Do you know what's down there?'

Frank found herself nodding. She hadn't meant to, but when had that stopped her admitting things?

'Good. Let us talk frankly then. We need to shut the leechway before someone else finds it. It's dangerous. I'll hold my hands up and admit it was my mistake agreeing to leave it open.' She looked away as she said this, as if she were talking to herself or to the world instead of to Frank. 'Will you do it? For me? For us all?'

'Do what?' Frank said. 'I don't understand what you're asking.'

'Take this,' the woman said, putting her dark glasses back on, opening her briefcase and pulling out a small metal disc.

She handed it to Frank. It was about the size of a chocolate digestive, but heavier.

'Take it down to the cellar and just put it on the ground. That's all. After that you can go. Then the next time the leechway opens it'll set the coagulant charge off –' she nodded at the disc in Frank's hand – 'and it'll all seal up as if there had never been an unplugged hole in the realities down there at all. No more leakage. No shadows, no smells, no dreams. No more risk. Simple.'

'I just saw one,' Frank said, not exactly changing the subject, and not exactly stalling for time, but just for something to say. 'A shadow with nothing casting it. In the garden, just now.'

'Oh, they're not usually anything to worry about,' Agent Jofolofski said. 'It'll just wander about for a bit, then fade away. Ten minutes, half an hour and they're gone if they're left alone. Trouble is not everyone leaves them alone, in the same way not everyone leaves a leechway alone. If you've got the right tools, the right abilities … it's bad news. So, take this –' she pointed at the metal disc in Frank's hand – 'and do as I ask.'

'I'm not sure,' Frank said. There were a lot of words to listen to, but something the woman hadn't said kept poking at her brain. 'This thing will take Nick's mum away, won't it? He'll never see her again?'

The woman sighed.

'Oh, child,' she said. 'You're right, he won't see her again, but this is more important than Nick and his mother. If this leechway isn't shut and soon, Bad Things will happen. Do you know what Bad Things are, little girl? They're not Good.' The woman was patronising Frank now. 'There are people out there, Bad People, who are always looking for these leechways between worlds.

People who'll take it and point it at some *other* other world. At somewhere more dangerous than where Nick's from. And it won't just be a window any more. They'll force it open and *let things out*. Dangerous things. You wouldn't want that, would you?'

'B-b-but it's been there for years,' Frank said. 'Nothing's happened. N-n-nothing's come out. It's just bouncing. Nick said so. Nick said y-y-you said so.'

'He talks too much,' the woman said, looking like a disappointed teacher. She went on, 'There are *ways* to open it again. And there are people, and things, out there who know how. Trust me on this.'

Frank believed her. She spoke as if she were sure of what she was saying, as if there really wasn't much time, as if Bad Things were about to happen, and Frank withered under her words. She shrivelled up inside. It was her fault that things had changed, that what had been normal and harmless for years and years was now broken and endangered.

She believed the woman, but she didn't like her.

'Look, just go back,' the woman said. 'Go back and drop this in the cellar and save the day, little girl. Save the world. It's easy. Simple. The Right Thing to do.'

'I can't,' Frank said, holding the metal disc out to the woman. 'I just can't. It's not right. You can't ask me to do it. It's not my place, not my secret. She's not my mum. I can't do that to Nick.'

Special Agent Jofolofski pulled her dark glasses off, rubbed the bridge of her nose and looked sadly at Frank.

For a moment she was silent, then she replaced her glasses, looked away and said softly, 'Keep it,' pushing Frank's hand away. 'Keep it, just in case.'

She opened the car door and climbed inside.

'I'll be back tomorrow, if there is one.'

Frank pulled her bike up on to the pavement as the woman drove off, turning right at the end of the street, by her school.

She thought about throwing the disc away, just forgetting it all, but instead she slipped it into her pocket. It felt heavy against her thigh, tugged down on her belt.

'Let's go home,' her stomach said, as if it had just come out from hiding.

'Where've you been?' she asked.

'Oh, nowhere,' it said. 'Nowhere.'

Frank wheeled her bike slowly along by the school field, along the pavement that led to the rec. She felt like she'd fallen through a hole in the floor of the normal world and into a spy film. Or was it a science fiction film? It certainly didn't feel like a comedy.

This woman – Auntie Mimi or Special Agent Jofolofski or whoever she was – wanted her to shut the window, wanted Frank to be the one to cut Nick off from his mum for good, and for what? To save the world from 'Bad People' because Noble had posted a video of the window online?

If Agent Jofolofski had really had the video taken off the internet, like Frank had overheard Nick's dad say, then what was the problem? It couldn't have been online for more than a few hours. Who'd've had a chance to see it?

Surely the secret was safe after all?

'Yeah,' said her stomach. (It had been listening in.) 'Of course it's safe now. Nothing's wrong at all. Everything is perfect. This is just a perfectly ordinary day.'

Sarcasm dripped on to the pavement in venomous little puddles.

She wheeled her bike towards the entrance to the park.

She didn't know what she was supposed to do. Her stomach was right, of course: you can't make an uncovered secret secret again. Nick's mum remained in danger, and Frank still hadn't told Nick the truth.

What should she do? What would be best for Nick? For her?

She wanted to turn around and go back to Nick's house. She wanted to tell him it was her fault, that she was the one who'd spilt the beans. She wanted to apologise and make it better. But then she felt the heft of the metal disc in her pocket and knew that the past couldn't just be put back the way it was, that an apology wasn't enough.

Frank was paying more attention to the pavement, and to the swirling insides of her head, than to the world around her. To her shock, and totally without warning, she was knocked to the ground by two hurtling figures.

The bike fell one way and she went the other, landing hard on her backside. She rolled on the damp pavement and ended up facing the way she'd come from, shaken but unhurt.

Looking up and rubbing grit off her hands, she recognised the backs of the two boys who'd knocked her down. It was Roy and Rob, or possibly Rob and Roy.

No apology was forthcoming, but there was no insult either, she remembered later, no smart Alec comment tossed over their shoulders. They just kept on running, as if knocking her down had been an accident, as if they'd hardly even noticed her. That was odd.

By the time she'd climbed to her feet, they'd gone, off round the corner. She'd never seen them move so fast. Didn't know they had it in them. They were thick-headed and thick-footed. They always reminded her of Frankenstein's monster, prodded into action, encouraged and sparked into life by Neil Noble's electric words. He pressed their buttons, pulled their strings, and they danced to his will.

So, what were they doing on their own? Running like that?

Neither she nor her stomach had an answer, but they were gone and it didn't look like they were coming back, so she started off again, heading for home.

As soon as she entered the park she realised something was wrong.

A smell like fireworks or bacon burning hung in the air, woven in with the usual scent of wet grass and anxiety.

A spider scuttled its cold feet down her spine and her stomach looked the other way.

A storm cloud was hanging over the rec. The rest of the park was sparkling in the afternoon sunshine, the grass glinting with raindrops, but no sun reached the swings or the slide or the roundabout. Just that one corner of the park was dark.

And there were voices.

Raised voices.

Naturally she looked; she couldn't help but turn and look that way, even though she'd immediately recognised one of them as Noble's voice and had no desire to look at *him*.

But for a moment she couldn't make sense of what she saw.

She could hear Neil arguing with someone. Could hear his voice, but she couldn't see him anywhere.

All she could see was a woman stood beside the roundabout, looking down at it.

She was young-looking, just a young mum with a smart pram, hair pulled back in a tight neat bun.

And then Frank blinked. There was something else.

It was as if she saw two pictures at once, two views of the world, one on top of the other, like when she had first seen Nick's mum in the cellar.

Where the woman stood, aping her posture, matching her gestures, was a thinner, blacker, more stick-man-ish, scarecrow-like figure. A pale blank face and fingers like twigs. Darkness hung over the rec again; shadows twisted around the thing's ankles.

And then Frank blinked again and all she could see, once more, was the perfectly normal-looking woman, and now she was standing up straight, turning around.

But where was Noble? Hiding in the shadows somewhere?

She had the oddest feeling that this woman, this young mum, was what Roy and Rob had been running from. That they hadn't just been in a hurry to get somewhere, that they'd been running in fear.

Had they seen what Frank had just seen? The stick-creature? Could they see the shadows? Did they understand what was happening?

Again the air shook, shuddered, and Frank saw what was supposed to be hidden, saw the ragged stick-creature, spiderish and sharp-edged. It loomed, pointing its flat, pale, almost blank face down at the floor of the roundabout, as if examining something.

Frank stood stuck to the spot and swallowed. She was terrified

in an entirely new way,
a better, braver way. This
thing wasn't just some stupid boy who
made her life hell; this was something entirely
other, something from a *real* nightmare. It was *right* to be afraid
of it.

And then she blinked and somehow the world was back to normal. The stick-figure was gone and in its place was the young woman, looking perfectly normal, perfectly human.

She didn't think she was going mad, just that some disguises are better than others. This thing-become-woman was clearly an expert. (When had Frank become so expert at noticing this weird stuff? When had it become normal to think about monsters and other worlds and shadows without stuttering?)

Her heart held its breath as the woman, pushing her pram, came out of the fenced off rec, looked at her and smiled.

And then, with one glance behind her, the woman pushed the pram up the path through the park towards the exit that led to Frank's estate. The opposite direction to Nick's house.

Frank breathed a sigh of relief at that. She was worried what would happen if this woman, this *thing*, found its way to the window in Nick's cellar, found his mum. Surely, Frank reckoned, that was what it was after Neil Noble for. His face had been in the video; it must've tracked him down somehow. It couldn't just be coincidence that a thing like this turned up in their rec at this particular moment, could it?

She wasn't the sort to judge books by covers or people by their appearances, but if this was the sort of thing that was hunting for the window, that wanted to control it, then perhaps Agent Jofolofski was right to be worried.

What are you doing?' her stomach said.

'Just taking a look,' she said.

Her hand was already on the metal latch of the little gate that led through the hip-high fence and into the playground.

'We should get home before it rains,' her stomach said.

She looked at the sky, now cloudless and deep blue. The shadows had gone.

'This'll only take a minute,' she said.

She had a curiosity that needed satisfying. She had to know where Noble was.

She walked slowly across the tarmac, eyes open, searching, looking.

The swings were empty and swayed restlessly in the occasional breeze. There was no one sat in the little shelter under the slide, no one sat on the bench beside the bin Rob had pulled that carrier bag of rubbish from, pretending it was Quintilius Minimus. That had been only a few days ago, but it seemed so much longer.

She wished Quintilius Minimus would show up now, that he'd just come strolling out of the shadows and explain to her what to do next. How she could help Nick.

But the cat didn't appear. Cats aren't to be relied upon.

She looked over at the nettles, the deep patch of rustling nettles that were the cause of all this trouble. If she'd just left her bag in there, then none of this would have happened … but she'd had enough of looking back and wishing things otherwise, enough of trying to find a place to lay the blame.

She stopped beside the roundabout. Noble wasn't here. He wasn't anywhere.

Trying to puzzle things out, she could only see two explanations. Firstly, that he'd never been there at all, that she'd imagined his voice, imagined the argument between him and the woman. Or, secondly, that he *had* been there but had somehow snuck away when she was distracted.

That second option seemed more likely, more realistic, but she was certain she would have noticed. There was nowhere he could have sneaked to. There was no secret way out of the playground. She would have seen him. Definitely.

So what had that stick-creature done to him?

And then she stopped thinking.

The roundabout, which she'd been absent-mindedly pushing, spun something odd into sight.

There was a dark stain on the wooden floor, shaped something like a person. Fuzzier, blurred, but clearly *personish*.

She reached out and grabbed one of the metal bars that divided the roundabout into sections. As she pulled it to a stop, battling its momentum, it tugged her a few steps along with it.

She staggered, but kept her footing.

When it was finally stationary she knelt on the damp boards and looked closer at the stain. She'd thought at first that it was water – a watermark or a puddle perhaps – but the whole of the wooden floor was wet; the old wooden planks were dark from the earlier rain. And it wasn't paint or oil or anything like that.

'It's just a shadow,' her stomach said. 'Let's go. Let's go now.'

Her stomach was right, she thought. It does look like a shadow. A person-shaped shadow.

Where her own shadow, cast by the sun, touched it, the two were indistinguishable; they were both shadows, just ordinary shadows. Except whereas she knew she was blocking the light to make the shadow shaped like her, there was nothing casting the other one. Nothing there at all.

'Normally they fade away,' Agent Jofolofski had said. But Frank had seen them rubbing round the stick-woman's legs purposely. As if they were working together somehow.

This shadow wasn't moving, but it *did* look person-shaped.

'You're an idiot for still being here,' her stomach said, looking the other way.

'I feel like I've fallen down a rabbit hole,' she said. 'The world is upside down and soon there's going to be a cake with "Eat me" written on it.'

She tried to distract herself from the inexplicable shadow by trying to recall what else happened in *Alice's Adventures in Wonderland*, but she couldn't remember. It had been her dad who'd read it to her. It was one of his favourites, but then he was a bit odd like that. Her mum laughed at him, not unkindly, because she preferred books without pictures.

'Wrong book,' said her stomach. 'It's *Peter Pan* where the shadow gets loose.'

Frank turned away, ignoring it.

She should just go home and lock the door and wait for Quintilius Minimus to turn up.

And then she heard a noise like balloons being squeezed together, like some clown making a balloon animal, but quieter, stranger, and she felt something cold move behind her, a shadow darting past the corner of her eye, and there was a gasping, choking noise and she spun back round to see, curled up and shivering on the damp wooden boards of the old roundabout, a boy.

He was white, not just his skin but his hair too. Even his clothes looked faded, washed out.

It was Neil Noble.

Frank was surprised and not surprised.

'I told you he was here,' she said to her stomach.

But she felt queasy.

Like the world was a ship.

And the afternoon was rocking.

Bobbing in a distant harbour.

And she was a new sailor.

And then she heard thin words whisper around her ankles. She couldn't make them out.

Noble was speaking.

She bent down.

'What did you say?' she said.

He spoke again.

He was almost inaudible, like he'd lost his voice on the morning of the school play, but she could just make out the words, 'I ain't no grass.'

'What do you mean?' she asked. 'What does that mean?'

He repeated it again, not looking at her, looking past her out into the distance.

'I-I-I ain't no g-g-grass.'

And then she laughed. In spite of everything, in spite of who he was, in spite of the glimpses of other worlds or other-worldly things she'd had, she laughed.

She understood what he was saying.

It was the language of the playground. That small defiance in the face of authority, the refusal to tell tales, to snitch, to get the teachers involved. You kept it among the kids, always, no adults allowed or needed.

He hadn't let on. Hadn't told tales. Hadn't spilt the beans.

She imagined it must have been a struggle for him, that choice between owning the secret himself and sharing it. If it was his alone then he could dangle it over Nick's head, send the ransom note letters, whisper cryptic hints when they were with other people, have his hurtful, hateful fun. But the moment it was out there, the moment someone else knew about it, then all his power would be gone. Was that how he thought?

But had he known what the woman was? (Whatever it was she was.) Had he seen what Frank had seen, seen the stick-thing behind the disguise? He couldn't have known all the things Frank knew, but maybe he suspected. Maybe deep down inside himself he knew it would be a bad idea to let the woman find the window …

Frank shook her head. Whatever the answer was, she was glad Neil had decided to keep mum.

'He did a better job of it than you,' her stomach reminded her, as if she hadn't already secretly thought the thought.

But now look at him … His hair was white, like a ghost or an old person. In fact, the whole of him looked washed out. What had the woman done? Where had he disappeared to? Trapped in a shadow?

That impossible shadow was gone now. Neil was casting one, but it moved with him, was quite normal. For a moment Frank thought about that, about where the shadow had run off to, why it had released him, but then she smelt a familiar sharp stink, and she let the question go. There was a dark patch on the front of Neil's trousers. He was shivering.

She couldn't leave him like this, could she? She wanted to run back to Nick's house and tell them what she had seen, warn them, save them, but she couldn't just leave Neil here.

'He'd leave you,' her stomach said.

'No, he wouldn't,' she said. 'Not if I was like this.'

'No, you're right. He'd crow. He'd sneer and point and prod you. And then he'd never let you forget that time you peed your pants at the playground.'

'That's not what I meant,' she said, even though she knew her stomach was probably right.

But what did that have to do with anything? This wasn't about him, was it? It was about her and who she wanted to be. She wanted to be a better person. Better than him at least. And not because it was a competition, just *because*.

She put a hand under his arm, tried pulling him up.

'I c-c-can't,' he said.

'Come on,' she huffed as she heaved.

He was wobbling up on to his feet. His eyes were dark and stared off into the distance.

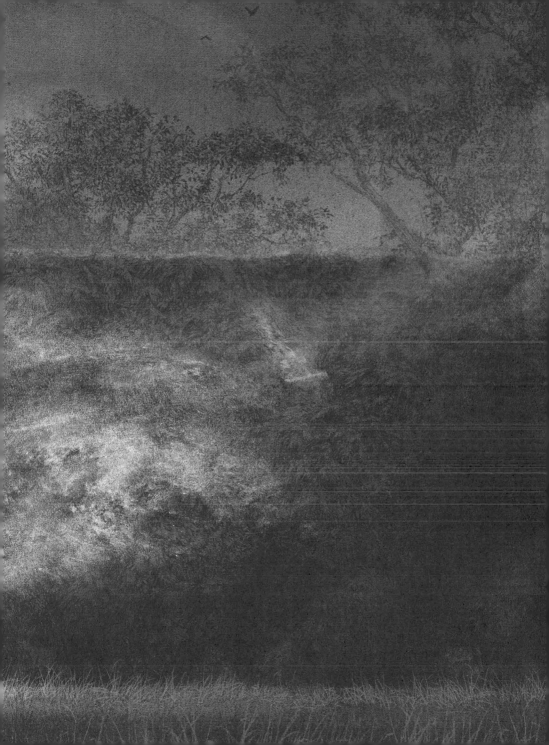

'Come on,' she said. 'Let's get you home.'

He leant on her shoulder and felt light, lighter than she'd ever imagined. Rob and Roy were the ones with the muscle, with the bulk. Neil was just the energy behind them, and now that had been drained away.

He was skinny under it all.

'W-w-where?' he said.

His trainers squelched as he moved.

'Get you home,' she repeated. 'Where do you live?'

She didn't know.

He didn't answer, but they lurched forward together, taking little steps, out of the rec and towards the park exit that led towards Nick's house.

It turned out he lived in the road before Nick's.

As they'd left the park and staggered round the corner into the street, he'd begun to regain some of his strength.

He'd been muttering, muttering in that distant, quiet whisper next to her ear, but she'd been unable to make out what he was saying. Just the odd word, fearful and confused.

She would have been lying if she denied that a tiny corner of her heart celebrated at the sight of him diminished and broken, but she wasn't proud of it. She wouldn't own up to it if she were asked, but she knew it was there and that there was a certain justice in it. But at the same time she was shocked by what had happened to him, terrified it might happen to her, or to Nick, or to anyone.

And then she felt the small weight of the boy lift off her as he staggered forward by himself, staggered off up a front path leading to a neat blue door beside which was a trellis with yellow roses growing on it. He pulled a set of jangling keys from his pocket and held them out at the door.

'Now can we go home?' her stomach asked. 'He's home. Look. Now it must be our turn. Yes?'

It was right. Frank had done what was needed. She could go home now, except …

Except that stick-creature, that scarecrow-woman was still out there, and Frank knew it was searching for Nick, for the window. She had to stop it.

'We're not going home,' she said to her stomach.

'But it's almost tea time,' her stomach said. 'I'm hungry.'

She looked at her watch. In fact it was barely even three o'clock.

'Dad's not expecting us back for another two hours,' she said. 'Plenty of time.'

'For what?' asked her stomach.

'We've got to warn them,' she said, and ran off, leaving Neil scratching the paintwork as he fumbled his key against the lock.

She ran, heading for the corner, heading for the next street along, and her shadow followed her, almost, but not quite, in time with her movements.

Frank went up the side of Nick's house, round to the back garden.

The back door was open.

Nick's bike was on the grass. There was an imprint beside it where hers had been.

She'd left it at the rec. Again.

It wasn't important though.

Looking up, she saw someone moving in an upstairs window next door. It was a semi-detached house, the two of them joined together with a shared wall. She wondered who lived next door: did they have a clue about what was happening?

Now that she knew the world was bigger, stranger, odder than she'd ever dreamt, she wondered what else she didn't know about. What happened in the house next door to her? What secrets did the other kids at school have?

She shook her head. This wasn't the time to be thinking; this was a time for doing and she had to go in and warn Nick and his dad about the thing that was looking for them.

But to do that, she thought, would be to admit to Nick that *she* had told his secret, wouldn't it? Could she tell him without letting that truth out? Did it really matter? He'd stop being her friend, but still she might save him.

If he and his dad went away before the thing found them, they'd be safe. Or if she could close the window like Agent Jofolofski had asked, maybe that would protect them too. But that would be Frank cutting Nick off from his mum, forever. How could she do that? How could she expect him to let her do that? How could she bear to see his face as she tried to do that?

It was all such a mess, and she was as good at juggling all the possibilities in her mind as she was at juggling flaming torches in real life. Which was 'not very'.

Her stomach chuckled to itself.

'If only you'd listened to me,' it said. 'None of this would've happened.'

And then she heard movement inside and she stopped thinking, stopped worrying, and went up the steps and into the kitchen.

As she did so a part of her shadow peeled off from the rest and lifted what might have been the shadow of a weasel-like nose with no weasel there to cast it. Like a shadow puppet on a screen it turned, sniffed the air, glanced at the cellar window and slid away round the side of the house and off to who knew where. Frank didn't notice feeling a tiny bit warmer, or if she did she just put it down to going indoors.

Nick's dad had just lifted the kettle up to pour steaming water into a mug.

'Frank,' he said.

'Where's Nick?' she asked.

He put the kettle down and looked at her. His eyes were grey with tiredness, even though it was only the early afternoon.

'He's just popped out,' he said. 'Just gone to the shops. He'll be back soon.'

It didn't ring true, and then Frank remembered that Mr Underbridge didn't know that she knew. Of course he wouldn't tell her the truth about where Nick was.

So she told Mr Underbridge about the thing she'd seen at the rec. She didn't tell him it was her fault or exactly who Neil Noble was. She mixed in some of the things Agent Jofolofski had told her. She told him what she knew. He listened in silence.

'Oh, Frank,' he said when she'd finished.

He sipped his tea.

'I don't know what to say,' he said. 'I'm sorry you got involved in all this. Nick should never have told you. It was supposed to be a secret. It was important.'

'It was my fault,' she said. 'I made him tell me. I heard the music and asked too many questions.'

He shook his head.

'He's not gone to the shops,' he said. 'We had an argument and he ran off. I thought he'd be all right if he had some time by himself. Time to cool down. I'm sure he'll be back soon. He always comes back.'

'I'm sorry,' Frank said.

'Don't worry. I'm not angry,' he said. 'Or not with you. Not with Nick, either. Mimi was right. She should have shut the window ten years ago. Right at the start.'

'We can do it now,' Frank said. 'She gave me a thing to put in the cellar. If the window's not there any more, the stick woman-thing won't ever find it, won't be able to do whatever it is she wants to do and you'll all be safe. Even if Nick's mum –'

'But we can't,' Mr Underbridge said. 'It's not just Nick's mum. It's Nick too. If the window to his home closes, he might …' His words trailed off.

'What?'

'What happens to a flower when it's plucked, or a leaf when it falls off the tree in autumn? As long as they're attached, just by a thread, they can grow. If Nick's world is severed, if his link to his home world, to where he was born, is cut, he might …'

'Die?' Frank asked.

'Yes,' he said. 'I think so. I couldn't do it … couldn't let her do it when he was just a baby. I certainly can't do it now. I love him too much.'

Guilt swelled in her throat and she could barely say, 'What do we do?'

'I don't know,' he said, mumbling. Then, 'I've got to find him.'

'I'll help you look,' she said. 'But first …'

It was almost embarrassing, but she needed to pee. You never read about this in books, she thought. No spy breaks off in the middle of a mission to use the loo; no wizard on a quest ever pops into a public convenience … But this wasn't a story: this was real life, admittedly a rather weird and surprising real life, but real life all the same.

She'd been running from one place to another all day, pinged around like that blasted metal ball in the pinball machine. But now she was alone for a minute, a moment's peace, and suddenly, sat there on the loo, the day caught up with her and her energy drained away. She was exhausted. Her fingertips hummed and she felt clammy and almost sick.

'It doesn't matter what he says,' her stomach said. 'It's all your fault. All of this. Oh! It's at times like this I wish I wasn't your stomach and was something with legs. My own legs. Then I'd be outta here.'

She didn't bother to answer because she knew it was right. Stomachs don't lie.

She thought back to the first time she'd used this toilet, when the music had come drifting up from somewhere below her, how it had buoyed her feelings up, lifted her out of the water and put her on dry land. She hadn't realised before then quite how long she'd been treading water, how exhausted she'd become. She wished the music would come again now, but it didn't; instead that nagging voice kept on talking.

'You heard him, he loves Nick, loves this weird stolen changeling child he's claimed as his own, never-you-mind where he comes from. And you're the one who let the secret slip, the one who's brought it all crashing down. It doesn't matter if that stick-woman-thing with the shadows turns up, it's going to be over for Nick one way or the other. Jofolofski's not going to leave the window open this time. You heard his dad. It's all going to be over for Nick soon, the whole of these past ten years a complete waste of time. He'll hate you. They'll both hate you. He'll –'

'Why are you saying these things?' Frank asked.

Her stomach was silent for a moment, then it said: 'You know I'm just *you*, don't you?'

The doorbell rang.

She looked up from her feet and stared at the back of the toilet door. It was blue, and she could see the brush strokes in the paint, swirling, waving like fingerprints, like the sea.

Mr Underbridge's footsteps hurried down the hallway.

Oh! Frank thought. *Nick doesn't have a front door key! Maybe …*

But when she heard the front door open there was no joyful, tearful reunion of dad and lost son, rather a voice she could barely make out, low and hushed, hidden, almost whispering.

'… car's broken down … can I use your … come in?'

'Oh,' said Mr Underbridge. (Frank could imagine the disappointment, confusion even, on his face.) 'Well, I suppose. But, why's –'

And then there was a sudden silence, cutting him off, and a darkness filled the hallway. Frank saw it through the crack underneath the toilet door. Where there had been a straight line of white light, a sudden night fell.

There was a thump, a thud, a noise like a scuffle, gasping breaths, a momentary groan, and then silence again.

The light came back.

Frank hardly dared breathe.

She thought of the shadow in the rec and on the roundabout.

Her stomach made no comment, firmly looking the other way, reading a newspaper, listening to loud music through big headphones.

If she made a noise, the woman (it *must be* the one from the park, mustn't it? Who else could it be? (Was it shaped like a woman, or like a stickman?)) would find her, and although she knew she wasn't what the woman was after, wasn't what the woman was looking for Frank didn't want to be the next thing she found. Not being that would be a Good Thing.

She wished Agent Jofolofski would turn up. She was someone who might be able to do something. But she wasn't coming back until the morning, with her warrant.

And what had happened to Mr Underbridge? Why wasn't

he talking? Why wasn't he fighting her off?

Silence ate her thoughts and spat out the memory of the shadow on the roundabout.

Hard-heeled footsteps clacked across the floorboards.

The footsteps came level with the toilet door and stopped.

Frank stopped breathing.

The woman walked off into the kitchen and Frank heard the cellar door swing open and the clicking footsteps fade away down the stairs.

After waiting another few moments, just to be sure the woman wasn't on her way back up, she eased open the toilet door and tiptoed into the hall.

The front door had been left open.

Frank stepped towards it, not knowing whether she was going to shut it or run for it.

She stopped.

There on the ground, just outside, was a pram lying on its side, the hood torn and flapping in the cool afternoon breeze.

The sun shone brightly and warmly. The concrete and mud of the world glowed, invitingly, washed in light.

'Look at that,' her stomach said. 'A beautiful sunny day! Let's go. It's over now. There's nothing you can do. Let's go home.'

But Frank knew she couldn't leave. Someone had to do something.

The black fabric of the pram hood flapped at her accusingly. A knitted white blanket was spilt on the step. The pram was empty.

It had never had a baby in it, she was sure of that much. Had it just been part of the woman's disguise, or had she carried something else in it?

As she watched, another shadow-with-nothing-to-cast-it slipped out from under the blanket, slim like a stoat or weasel, and slid across the earth.

Watching it was like hearing two balloons rub together, and the smell of far-off crackling fireworks drifted through the air.

It darted at her, touching her toes, her sandalled foot, covering it in its darkness, slipping back and letting her go, before sliding forward again.

Her foot was numb, like it was falling asleep; she wobbled as she tried to step backwards.

This thing had been left to guard the house, to stop people coming in … or going out.

It slid up her leg, higher this time. It was like stepping into a cold bath, but dry, bone dry.

It was so odd to see. There was nothing there, nothing attacking her, nothing she could fight against, nothing to get her fingers round or her nails into. It was just her leg in shadow.

Nevertheless, she tried brushing it away, but her fingers just went over the top, did nothing.

She tried stepping back. The shadow had stretched itself up to her thigh now and her leg gave way. She fell, banging her bum on the doorstep.

She should cry out, she thought, but what good would that do? Who could help her? Even if someone heard her, what could they do?

She felt oddly calm, shocked into calmness by the slow, cold, smooth strangeness of the attack.

Fingers of shadow were reaching on to her other leg now too. Where she'd fallen, her legs had touched one another and the shadow was creeping across her jeans like spilt water.

She rolled over and, using her arms, dragged herself half into the hallway. But it was no good. There was no rescue waiting in there. If Mr Underbridge could help, he'd've been there by now; he'd've done something.

And then the cold was gone and her legs, no longer numb, just hurt. Sharp, stabbing, tingling, awful pain, but at least she recognised it as a normal stage in that progression from numbness to pins and needles to excruciatingness back, eventually, to ordinary-legness.

With an effort she rolled over on to her back and half sat up.

Quintilius Minimus was sat in the front garden. It had one leg up in the air and was washing unmentionable parts.

Scattered on the earth around it, moving like earthworms, were thin slivers of darkness, the strange remains of a shredded shadow.

As she looked, the cat looked up at her, the tip of its tongue stuck out. It held her eyes for a moment before rolling over on to all four feet, lifting its crooked tail in the air and jumping on to the garden wall.

It began washing its shoulder.

She heard the words from the other night echo in the back of her head: 'Harmless. Taste of nothing.'

'Thank you,' she said, forgetting that those are two words cats do not understand.

The cat, being just a cat, said nothing.

In the hallway, to the left of the kitchen door, there was a short bit of wall, maybe the length of a ruler, a foot wide, before it turned the corner.

The hall was white and light, and sun shone in from the open front door behind Frank, from the landing window above and from the kitchen.

But that corner.

The corner of the hall by the kitchen door was filled with shadows.

They moved as she looked at them. There was nothing in the hallway to cast them, no hatstand, no person. But still they shifted and flicked as if a breeze she couldn't feel was blowing something she couldn't see.

Against her best judgement, but swallowing all fear

deep inside her, she tiptoed forward.

The soft soles of her sandals were silent on the floorboards.

As she got closer to the corner she could see more shape.

The shadows were flat against the wall, just a place where the light didn't reach, but there was something inside them, something that she could see *through* them. And then the wall bulged a little, seemed to shift as well.

She saw a smudge of a face.

It was Mr Underbridge, as she'd feared, as she'd expected. He'd been swallowed by shadows, wrapped up by them, pinned against or in or on the wall, like a caterpillar that had wrapped itself up in silk in between two beams in the attic or on the underside of a leaf.

She reached a hand out to touch the wall where the shadows lay, where Nick's dad was hidden, but stopped herself short. Her leg went cold at the thought.

What she thought were Mr Underbridge's eyes, far away in the darkness, charcoal in charcoal, grey under grey, begged her to run, and she wished she could listen to him.

And then, creeping in at the edges, came the music. The worlds were bumping together. The window had appeared again. But this time the stick-creature was in the cellar.

Oh, she thought, *where's Nick?*

She eased open the cellar door, thankful for its silent hinges.

The music washed around her feet, whispered in her heart, quieted the continual grumbling of her stomach. It felt like the opposite of the shadows, sort of. As if she were being filled with an anti-pins-and-needles, as if she was walking in sunlight, not shade.

But she didn't feel brave, not exactly. Her heart was a butterfly and her legs still wobbled, not from the after-effects of the shadow's touch, but from real fear. Just because she was afraid, though, was no reason to not get on with it.

What it was exactly that she could do, she didn't know. But she had to do it now.

Halfway down the wooden stairs, just before they turned the corner, one step creaked, a sharp and intrusive noise, not like the music, something quite other. She stopped, hoping against hope the stick-woman hadn't heard it.

Nothing happened.

Frank crouched down and peered between the banisters.

The cellar was filled with the light of the other world. There was Nick's mum, working at her desk, weaving threads of melody together, hushing some, raising others, harmonising and modulating, rewinding and replaying.

She was beautiful, Frank saw: huge and grey and lumpen, mossy behind the ears and undeniably trollish, but beautiful too. She could see Nick in her, and her in Nick.

But in front of the vision of the other world, firmly and spikily in *this* world, was something else, something un-beautiful, something that smelt rotten to look at.

The young mum she'd seen in the park, who'd wheeled her pram to the front door, was gone. Gone for good now, Frank reckoned. This time she couldn't just blink and make the unworldly go away. The stick-creature scarecrow-thing didn't care about disguises any more. Not here. Not now. Unimportant.

The face was chalk white, flat, cloth-like, the mouth a narrow slit in the blankness, the eyes burning blue dots. She was stretched out and narrow, thin and dandling, like a stick insect who listened to too much heavy metal. Like a withered mummy wrapped in bandages of shadow, black and dark and waving in invisible breezes.

How many limbs she had, Frank couldn't be sure. One moment

it looked like just the two arms, but then she seemed to be making too many movements with her hands. They were here, and here, and here, and here, and *here*, and there seemed to be no time between them. There was something sharply spiderish about her, about *it*, as if this *thing* were sat in the middle of its web, as if the world were its web and Frank was a fly who hadn't realised just how stuck she was. Not until now.

In front of it was a box on top of a tripod, a machine of some sort that buzzed and clunked like a bike that wouldn't change gears.

The thing fiddled with switches and buttons, and made movements with its twig-like, pincer-like hands in the air, leaving shimmering lines in front of it, like on a TV show where the presenter, a jolly idiot in a jumper, writes the number of the week with his finger, leaving a computer-generated digit behind on the screen. But these weren't numbers. They were symbols, letters, strange shapes from forgotten alphabets, that shimmered, faded and were gone.

What was it writing? What was it doing? Was it a spell of some kind?

It looked back at the machine on top of the tripod, adjusted something and the clunking sound stopped, replaced by a smooth, regular ticking and a low hum like something in tune. (Not in tune with the music, which swirled and leapt, always one step ahead, but in tune with itself, which was good enough.)

Nick's mum looked up from her desk and seemed to see the stick-creature. She looked shocked or saddened or surprised. Frank couldn't read the expression on that wide head easily, but then the troll looked up at her, blinked twice with those grey eyes and smiled. Frank was sure of *that*.

And then the troll composer vanished.

The music vanished.

Frank felt sick, as if all the worlds had just heaved themselves up over a humpback bridge at high speed.

'Uh-oh,' her stomach said, threatening to revisit its contents through her mouth.

Frank gripped the railings of the banister tighter and watched.

The window, or leechway, as Jofolofski had called it, was still there – Frank could see the mistiness – but it had suddenly turned away from Nick's world, from Nick's mum's world, and pointed *somewhere else*.

There was dust.

Grey dust.

Slowly moving grey dust.

It sounded like a distant seashore, something shifting, like far-off shingle sucked back by the waves, but constantly, never letting up. On and on the faint noise rolled.

Dust filled the cellar, like but unlike fog, just as Nick's mum's room had a moment before. Frank could still see the boxes and abandoned odds and ends of this world beyond, behind and through the dust, but …

The music was gone, and the loss of it was a stone across her shoulders.

This new world wasn't a place where music came from. It looked to be a grey place, broken and lost. A world long past its sell-by date.

Although Frank had been told that only light and sound came through the window, the cool foresty smell of Nick's house had gone, replaced with something like raw meat – faint, just at the edges, but days-old meat.

Somewhere she heard a fly buzz, but couldn't tell if it was real or in her mind.

And then something moved.

Something moved in this *other* other world.

It was another thin stick-man of a person, scribbled black lines of limbs and sharp blue glowing eyes.

It approached from far off in the dust, far off beyond the cellar.

Closer and closer.

Time stretched out, like space.

Frank didn't breathe.

And then the scarecrow stick-person stopped; it was as close now as Nick's mum had been, elsewhere, but within the walls of the cellar.

The dust roiled around it, and the creature chittered.

Just as a cat chitters at a bird through a window, longing to get out there and … well, *play* with the bird, its soon-to-be new best friend. But every bird knows that playing with a cat rarely marks the beginning of a long-lasting friendship. Birds are fragile things, and cats don't know their own strength.

The stick-creature that was here already, in this world, in the cellar, chittered back across the divide between them.

They were talking to one another.

It was a conversation.

They were the same. Not the same person, but the same sort of *thing*, the same species.

It was obvious now she thought it.

Frank gulped.

Behind the new stick-creature, she saw more of them coming forward, stepping into view through the swirling dust. There wasn't just one waiting for the window, there were many.

Their blue eyes glowed: four, eight, sixteen, more. They trailed off into the distance, far beyond the bounds of the cellar, back into the endless grey dust storm of their overlapping world, these shrouded, chittering stick-folk.

They wanted out.

They wanted *in*.

Frank didn't know what to do.

She was alone at the far edge of the world, looking out as though from the crow's nest of a ship. She wanted to shout down to the captain, let them know that she'd seen a Jolly Roger flying on the horizon. But she had no captain to hear her when she shouted. She was all alone as she sailed on. Just her.

Jofolofski's metal disc was cold in her pocket. It was heavy.

She could throw it. Push the worlds apart and shut the window for good. But …

It shouldn't have been her down in the basement making these decisions. This was one time when she'd happily have thrown her hands up and said, 'But I'm just a kid,' – if only there were a grownup nearby who'd listen.

The world she could see into looked horrible. What had happened to it? Just dust and dust and more dust. Even the light there seemed dim, seemed shadowed and cold and weak. It limped between dust grains, never quite summoning the energy to really *shine*.

It was a world at the end of its life.

Maybe these people … because that's what they were, wasn't it? No matter how they looked, they were *people*, like Nick was, like she was, like Nick's mum was … Maybe these people were just looking for a new world, one with sunshine and fresh air …

Maybe they came in peace. She wanted, in spite of everything she'd seen, to believe that.

But then she thought of Mr Underbridge writhing in the shadows upstairs. She thought of Neil Noble shuddering on the roundabout, damp-trousered and terrified. She remembered the feel of that thing on her leg and she thought of Agent Jofolofski's words.

What could she do?

'Give up,' said her stomach.

She didn't listen.

There was a noise upstairs, up in the kitchen.

She heard the back door slam shut and she turned to look up the stairs.

Behind her the stick-creatures were chittering to each other, as the one in this world fiddled with the contraption on the tripod.

The machine began to hum a different note. Lower, deeper, more certain.

Instantly the cellar filled with a warm breeze, dry and dusty and smelling reddish and rotten with meat and flies and strange spices.

Frank gasped, choked on it. She held back a cough.

That was the air of *another world*. The window was open.

Glancing back down into the cellar, she saw a small circle suspended in the air, ringed with flickering orange light. Through it, the dust world and the figures in it looked more real, more solid, more *there*. Outside the circle they were still transparent, visions through which the cellar could still be seen.

The hole, the opening, was small, but it was growing bigger.

'Dad?' shouted a voice from upstairs.

Nick had come back. He'd come home.

She wanted to shout for him, but didn't dare.

The wind from that other world whistled through the cellar, a high-pitched drone, monotonous and hopeless.

Footsteps thumped across the cellar ceiling, across the kitchen floor, and light burst in at the top of the stairs.

Nick's head poked round the corner.

'What's that noise?' he asked, to himself or to the world. He wasn't expecting to find Frank, and his eyes went wide as she scuttled up a few steps towards him.

'Quick,' she said. She didn't know what else to say. How could she find enough words to explain what was going on, to tell him the danger, to make him see that the window was open to another world, that it had to be shut, and that she had a thing in her pocket that would do it.

And then, just for a second, just for a second and a half, she heard the music, Nick's mum's music, sweep through the house.

Nick came galumphing down the stairs as she looked over her shoulder.

The machine on the tripod was crackling, little orange sparks flickering across it. The stick-figure was fiddling with it, adjusting knobs and chittering angrily.

The grey dust storm was gone and there was sunlight. From where she was squatting Frank saw the corner of the music computer, saw the edge of Nick's mum's elbow, and then … it flickered away with a crackle, like a needle dragged off an old record, and the dust was back, filled with those *things* with their glowing blue eyes and their hungry, thin bodies.

'What on earth – !' shouted Nick.

And the thing turned and fixed him with its eyes and reached out with one of its claw-like, stick-like arms and snatched him, big as he was, off the stairs and dangled him in the air.

Nick wriggled like a fish. Behind him, Frank (creeping a few steps lower for a better view) saw that the circle of clarity, that opening in the window, was getting bigger. Not big enough for the others to climb through yet, but not far off.

It wouldn't be long before these things started coming out of the dust and into her world.

'Get off me!' Nick shouted, flailing out with his arms.

Big as he was though, he couldn't reach the thing that held him up. Its companions, its fellow stick-folk in the dust chittered and clacked.

The thing turned and chittered back. Talking.

'Nick,' Frank hissed.

He twisted to look at her.

'Frank,' he said. 'I'm so sorry. I'm so sorry about all this. It's *my* fault.'

He gestured with his arm at *everything*.

Frank was amazed.

Here he was, hanging upside down in the claw of some

monster, with a portal to another world opening behind him,
and he was apologising to *her*.

'What an idiot,' her stomach said.

She took a deep breath and, ignoring that voice inside her,
said, 'Nick. It's opening the window. Opening it like a door. It's
going to let all its … *friends* through. That's not good.'

'No,' Nick agreed. (How calm he was, how calm he seemed!)
'I don't like the look of them very much. And although you
shouldn't judge books by their covers …' He left the end of the
sentence dangling, like he was.

As ridiculous as the situation was, she smiled. He wasn't
afraid. Or if he was afraid he wasn't letting her see it. Her heart
pulsed with feeling for him.

Here they were, very possibly at the end of the world, and he
was making jokes.

The stick-creature was ignoring them. Although it held a tight
grip around Nick's ankle, it wasn't looking at them: it was talking
to the other world; it was watching the circle of clarity, the way in,
the door grow slowly wider. (One of its companions was poking
a blank face through, its slit-mouth opening to taste the air of the
cellar.)

They were no threat to it.

'Agent Jofolofski gave me a *thing*,' Frank said. 'A thing to close
the window.'

'Then use it.'

'*For good*,' Frank said. 'It'll close the window *for good*.'

'Do it.'

For a fraction of a second the shushling drone of the dust storm became a melody and the grey light of the scarecrow-world sparkled with sunlight as the machine on the tripod groaned and sparked … but then it was back.

'I can't,' Frank said. 'If the window cl–'

'I know,' he said, cutting her off.

And that was it. Nick had spoken.

He understood.

He began struggling again in the thing's grip, trying to wriggle free or, Frank realised, to distract it while she did what she had to do.

Frank pulled the heavy metal disc from the pocket of her jeans.

It didn't look anything special. There were no buttons or dials to fiddle with. Just a peeling paper label: *Govt Issue Coagulant Charge Mk III (medium) – £50 fine for Misuse.*

'Put it down and get out of the way before the leechway appears,' Agent Jofolofski had said. It was open now, wide open and getting wider. She just had to throw it. That would work, wouldn't it?

She was a rubbish thrower, but it was only a few metres away, and she was halfway up the stairs. It would be easy.

Underarm.

Just a gentle lob up in the air and it would land in the middle of that dust cloud, a dust cloud filled, thronged, packed with stick-men and stick-women, all clacking and chittering, all waving their many arms urgently, black and shadowy, sharp and scary. Blue-eyed. Pale-faced. Hungry.

'Get on with it,' her stomach said.

And she threw the charge.

A metal disc, about the size of a digestive biscuit, but somewhat heavier, span, end over end, through the air towards the mouth of another world …

… and was snatched from the air by a narrow, pincer-like, twig-like hand.

Nick fell to the floor with a crash.

The slit-mouthed face twisted on its stiff neck to look at

what it had caught. It seemed to read the label carefully before turning to peer directly into Frank's soul.

She trembled, shivered, panicked and tried to scurry back up the stairs.

All was lost. The stick-creature stabbed a long arm between the banisters and grabbed her ankle. It tugged and Frank fell, banging her grazed knee on the step. She yelped, without meaning to.

She scrabbled with her fingernails on the bare wood of the stairs, but was dragged backwards until her foot was pulled tight against the banister. Then, with a sharp tug, she was yanked into the air.

And there she dangled, held like Nick had been.

She saw him on the floor below her, crawling away, staggering to his feet.

Dozens of blue lights peered at her from that swirling grey land of dust. They seemed as curious as the thing that held her.

'Chitter, chitter, chitter,' they said.

She was swung round, wriggling, to face her captor, loose change slipping out of her pockets and tinkling to the ground. Her top was falling down (or maybe up – towards her face at any rate) and she was keeping it in place with one hand while reaching out with the other for the disc-shaped charge in the creature's stick-fingered claw.

She couldn't reach.

Shadows curled around the walls. Frank heard clicking footsteps and saw that one of the stick-people had climbed into the cellar. Another one had its leg hooked out of the window and was ducking to slip its head through too.

The circular opening was *just* wide enough now.

'Mum!'

It was Nick's voice.

Frank twisted and caught a glimpse of him standing at the foot of the stairs.

He was looking at Frank, looking at the thing holding her, looking at the mechanical apparatus on the tripod that hummed softly as it somehow forced open the hole.

'Mum!' he shouted again.

It was as if he wanted her to hear him, wanted her to look at him. But she was in another world, one that was no longer touching this one.

'She can't hear you,' Frank said, almost to herself.

But it had been enough to get the stick-creature holding her to look his way.

It seemed puzzled, and it chittered at its companion who stood beside it.

'Now, Frank,' Nick said.

And she looked and saw that the thing's clawed hand was lowered, was idling in the air, and she wriggled and grabbed at it, gripping the wrist with one hand and wrapping her other hand round the metal disc.

She snatched and it came free.

With a spitting noise the stick-creature let her fall before she could throw it and she hit the ground with a hard *crump*. And then the rising, whistling sound of the grey dust-wind once again merged into music, and Frank knew, without looking round, that the window had shifted back again, that Nick's mum was back.

The box on the tripod groaned, whistled, sparked.

Something black and withered like a burnt log fell to the ground beside her. It was the leg, or most of the leg, of the stick-creature that had been climbing out of the opening when the worlds had swapped.

She heard angry hissing voices and thundering footsteps and a noise like an impact, and she rolled on to her back, looked up just in time to see the mountainous shape of Nick slam into the first stick-creature, the one from the park, and propel it forward, both of them hurtling through the glowing circle and into Nick's mum's studio.

They rolled together on the floor and Frank saw the troll woman get up from her instrument and step towards them. The stick-creature looked so thin and frail, so raggedy compared to her, Frank almost wondered what she'd ever been afraid of.

She could see Nick's mum's studio more clearly through the open window – it was a summer house and green gardens were visible through a doorway at one side – and she watched helplessly as Nick and the stick-creature rolled and wrestled across the floor.

(Did she dare jump through the open window herself? How could she help?)

Nick's mum reached down and, with surprisingly delicate fingers, lifted the stick-thing up into the air and peered at it. With the other hand she pulled Nick to his feet.

Without letting go of the creature, but holding it out to one side, she turned to look at Nick. Her eyes were wet and her cave-like mouth quivered.

Nick stepped forward. As tall as he was, she towered over him.

As they embraced – his arms timidly touching her waist, one of her hands covering his back, the other hand dangling the wriggling stick-creature off to one side – the scene began to fade.

Frank saw that there was a shimmering darkness glowing in Nick's hand, like a candle flame but the opposite, in negative.

She looked down at her hand. It was empty; the floor around her was empty. Nick had snatched up the metal disc, Agent Jofolofski's coagulant charge, and taken it with him through the doorway-in-the-window.

'Nick!' she shouted. 'Quick! Come back.'

As the darkness grew around him, his mum looked up, looked at Frank through the open space of the orange-rimmed window, heard her shouting. She let go of Nick.

'Nick!' Frank shouted again.

Her heart was banging. The flame of darkness surrounding the disc was growing. It was getting hard to see.

She scuttled to the stairs, where they'd sat and watched the other world through the window together. She'd be safe there, far enough away from the closing, overlapping worlds.

She looked back and saw Nick's mum kneeling down beside him. She gently bumped her huge forehead against his, touched his hand where the dark spark flared, and pushed him.

'Nick,' Frank yelled, 'get out of –'

But her sentence was cut off as darkness engulfed the whole scene, obliterated the window, vanished Nick's mum's world back into elsewhere with a great crashing noise that sounded like boxes falling over.

Then the darkness faded and faint sunlight poured in from above.

The connection was shut, severed, done. For good.

There was a sound like a coin spinning on tiles, but duller and heavier, which slowed and fell to silence with a solid *thunk*.

The cellar was just a cellar again, filled with the things that end up in cellars and attics the world over. Boxes and forgotten toys and furniture.

And dust.

The hard floor was covered with a grey dust that smelt of far-off deserts.

And in the middle of it was the burnt-out shape of the metal disc Nick had taken with him into his mother's world.

The machine on the tripod whined, whirred, coughed, sparked and finally rumbled to a halt, and the scarecrow-like thing, the one that had stepped through the door and was new to this world, stood and stared at the place where the window had been. It too had been beyond the window's reach when it had been sealed shut.

Its shoulders hunched. The glowing blue eyes didn't dim, but flickered. It chittered a few short words, then stood silent.

It didn't seem to know what to do now.

Frank edged away into the corner of the stairs. The hard wall against her back was good. Solid.

Nick had gone.

Nick had *gone.*

She couldn't believe it.

'Believe it,' her stomach said. 'The idiot went and did it.'

The doorbell rang upstairs.

She glanced at the stick-person, but it wasn't moving.

She pulled herself to her feet and climbed the stairs, feeling nothing.

There was knocking at the door now, as well as ringing.

As Frank went into the hallway she looked at the shadow-patch by the kitchen door. She had hoped that the shadows would release Mr Underbridge when the thing that had commanded them was gone from the world. But they hadn't.

She felt sick.

What had just happened was catching up with her.

Nevertheless, she pulled herself up to her full height, wiped some dust off her cheeks and opened the front door.

On the other side was Special Agent Jofolofski.

'Look, I got this through extra quick.' She waved a bit of paper. 'You're going to have to –'

She stopped when she saw it wasn't Mr Underbridge.

'Ms Patel,' she said coolly. '*You're* here. I didn't expect that.'

'It's done,' Frank said.

Special Agent Jofolofski nodded.

'Well done,' she said. 'I know how hard this must've been for you –'

'It's done,' Frank said. 'But it's not over. I need your help.'

She stood back to let the agent in and pointed towards Mr Underbridge.

Looking around as she walked, sniffing the air and stepping carefully, Agent Jofolofski made her way over to the corner and examined the shadow.

It shifted like the shadow of a swimmer at the bottom of a sunlit pool.

'Ms Patel,' she said. 'Hold this for me.'

She gave Frank her briefcase and snapped open the catches. Lifted the lid. Pulled out an aerosol canister. Gave it a shake.

'They're just nuisances, these things,' she said, as she sprayed the can at the wall. 'Mostly harmless. They usually fade away soon enough, unless someone finds them first.'

The shadows shrivelled up as she sprayed them and Mr Underbridge fell to the hall floor, choking and coughing on the fumes.

He was pale and shaking. He looked cold, his fingers blue, as though he'd been trapped under the ice. Like Neil his hair had turned white, although it had been going that way already, and his clothes were faded.

'Frank,' he croaked, looking up. 'And … you?'

Special Agent Jofolofski knelt down and put her arm round him.

'Yes, it's me,' she said.

'Where's Nick? Has he come back yet?'

'I don't know,' she said, looking up at Frank.

'The troll-boy's gone,' her stomach said.

'I'm so sorry,' Frank said. And then she remembered. 'There's a *thing* in the cellar.'

But when Special Agent Jofolofski tiptoed down the stairs all there was was mid-afternoon sunlight from the high windows and a smooth covering of thick dust everywhere. She scooped some of it into a little plastic bag and put the burnt-out disc back in her briefcase.

Frank described what the thing had looked like as best as she could.

Jofolofski listened closely, nodded and picked up the stick-like leg that had been left behind.

'But where's Nick?' Mr Underbridge said, still shaky, still unsure of what had happened.

How could Frank tell him? What exactly could Frank say? That Nick had been the hero who'd stopped a … what? An invasion? Or that he'd gone back to his mum? Would that make his dad feel better? She didn't know. Words failed to find her mouth and she just stood there.

'Perhaps we should put the kettle on,' Jofolofski said, seeing Frank's face. 'I think we need a cup of tea.'

But then there was a noise as boxes of junk fell in the corner of the cellar and a great shape lurched out from under them.

'Nick?' Mr Underbridge said.

'Hi, Dad,' said Nick, sounding strangely sheepish. 'I'm … I'm sorry.'

His dad ignored the apology, not needing it, and hobbled over to hug his son.

Frank stared.

'I thought he was *gone*?' her stomach said.

'Yes,' she replied. 'I thought so too, but he's not. He's still here.' Upstairs Frank and Nick sat with the two grownups and tried to explain exactly what had happened.

'When the thing went off,' Nick said, meaning the disc that closed the window, 'she pushed me out of the way. Quite a shove. She sent me flying into the cellar, into those boxes. I don't think she knew her own strength.'

'She sent you home,' Frank said.

'I guess so,' he replied, with a strange mixed look on his face.

Once they'd finished answering questions, Special Agent Jofolofski turned to Frank and said, 'Thank you for your courage and for your help, Ms Patel.'

'But I didn't do anything,' Frank said. 'It was Nick who did it.'

'No,' Nick said, shaking his head. 'That's not it at all.'

'Team effort?' offered his dad.

'Not even that,' said Nick. 'Not exactly.'

Special Agent Jofolofski shook her head.

'Let's not worry too much about where to lay the praise. Let me just say that His Majesty will be most grateful to both of you for your cooperation and assistance in this matter. It is also my duty to inform you that you are bound to silence about what has happened here this afternoon and on all concomitant subjects, observations and phenomena. There are forms you are obliged to sign, the Unofficial Secrets Act and so on.'

When Frank walked in the back door an hour later, her dad turned from the fish pie he'd just pulled out of the oven and said, 'Aha! Darling, you're just in time!'

'That smells nice,' she said.

'Thank you. I made it myself.'

She picked the cardboard packet up off the side and read, '"Fifty minutes at gas mark —"'

'And how was *your* afternoon,' her dad interrupted. 'Do anything fun?'

'Well …' she said, thinking about it. 'We just watched TV for a bit and played some more Swingball. That's all.'

(Frank realised later that she should have just told him the truth, the whole truth and nothing but the truth, so that they could've had one of those funny moments you see in films, where the kid says, 'I defeated dark forces and saved the world,' and the parent, not really listening, just says, 'Jolly good.' But things like that rarely happen in real life.)

'Jolly good,' her dad said, taking some garlic bread out of the oven. 'Smell that,' he said. 'Beautiful. I made it all myself.'

She picked up a wrapper from the side and read, '"Six minutes at –"'

'You should go next door,' he interrupted. He meant into the living room.

'Why?'

'There's someone there you might want to see.'

That was odd, Frank thought. Had Jess come back from holiday early or something?

She went through to the lounge. Hector was sitting in the middle of the floor with his Lego spread out around him. And there, sat on the arm of the sofa, watching him carefully, was Quintilius Minimus.

'He just turned up about ten minutes ago,' her dad called from the kitchen. 'Strolled in bold as brass as if nothing had happened.'

The cat looked up at her, its odd coloured eyes blinking slowly as though pleased with the way everything had turned out.

When they'd first spoken, the cat had called the window 'a problem', and now the problem had been dealt with. Frank had done what the cat had wanted, like people always seem to do with cats.

Her heart beat loudly in her ears as she tried to hug him and he tried to escape.

'You came home,' she said, stating the obvious.

When Frank went to bed that night she lay awake with her head buzzing.

It wasn't fear that was keeping her awake though.

After what she had been through, after what she had seen and done, she couldn't imagine any possible world out there in which Neil Noble would be a problem.

'Maybe, maybe,' her stomach said, not entirely getting into the spirit of things.

Her thin curtains did little to keep out the last of the sunshine, and through the open window she could hear the muffled sounds of voices from a party a few gardens away.

'Francesca?' It was her mum, home late from work. 'You asleep?'

'No, Mum,' Frank said.

'Did you have a good day? Been busy?'

'Yes. Nick and I saved the world.'

'Really? How did you do that?'

She sat down on the edge of the bed, right where Quintilius Minimus would curl up later on.

And so Frank told her mum the story of the last few days (leaving out most of the Neil Noble bits, because it was her story and why shouldn't she?) and her mum laughed and gasped and finally said, 'Goodness, darling, after all that you ought to sleep well.'

It was only when her mum had gone that Frank remembered the paperwork she'd signed, the promises she'd made to Special Agent Jofolofski and the king and the government. She hoped her mum hadn't taken her story too seriously.

FRIDAY AND ONWARDS

The following morning Frank met Nick over at the rec.

They sat on the swings and for a while swayed gently back and forth.

There was no sign of Neil Noble or his goons.

Frank said what had been on her mind, what her stomach had been telling her.

'It was all my fault.'

'What?'

'Everything. It was me who told Noble about your mum, about the cellar.'

'I know that,' said Nick. 'Who else could it have been? It doesn't matter.'

'What? Of course it matters,' she said.

'Why? Did you tell them on purpose?'

'No! Of course not. They made –'

'Then how could it matter? We both knew they were unpleasant idiots to begin with. They did something unpleasant. Well, there's no surprise there, is there?'

'But if I hadn't told them, then the window would never have been shut, and ...'

'I'd still have my mum?'

'Yes.'

'I hugged her, Frank,' he said slowly, not looking at her. 'I got to touch her, and even though it was only a moment, only a few seconds, she held me. I never imagined that would happen. Never in my most unlikely dreams. And it was good. She was cool and soft, Frank. And she knew who I was. I was always afraid she didn't know. But she knew.'

He stopped talking and sighed. Frank didn't look at him in case he was crying.

Then he went on. 'I hugged my mum, Frank, after all these

years. For the first time. And I've got you to thank for that.'

She laughed. Nervously, shyly.

'But the window's shut,' she said, after a moment.

'Oh, but I've still got her, Frank.' He tapped his chest like someone in a schmaltzy Hollywood movie who says, 'She'll always be in my heart.' He didn't say that though. Instead he just said, 'I can remember the music. I can remember her. It's not ended.'

They swung in silence for a few moments.

There were still things that bothered Frank.

'Your dad told me,' she said, 'that Special Agent Jofolofski had told him that if the window was shut that you … you might not …' She didn't want to say the word.

'We're talking about other worlds, about weird and spooky stuff, Frank,' Nick said. 'I guess no one knows *exactly* how it all works.'

'So you knew you'd be OK?' she asked.

'Of course not,' he said. He paused. 'I don't know though. I think I feel different now. It's hard to say, but since the window was shut, I've felt different. Maybe something's changed.'

Frank wondered if that meant he'd stopped growing, or stopped growing like a troll. Life would be awfully awkward if he ended up as tall as his mum.

'I've made a promise,' Nick said. 'I haven't told anyone, but I'll tell you.'

Frank looked at him.

'There was a window in my cellar, wasn't there? And that stick-creature thing was looking for these windows. Well, when I grow up, or grow up a bit more – you know, after we're done with school, or maybe in the holidays – I'm going to look for them too. If there was *one* window, there must be more out there somewhere. I'll find her. One day, I'll see her again, Frank. If I can I'll get back across to her. Somehow. I promise.'

Frank was witness to this promise and she knew that he meant it.

She heaved herself forward in the seat and started swinging higher.

Time went on.

Jess came back from her holiday and was shocked when Frank told her she'd made friends with Nick Underbridge. They didn't talk for days, but Frank didn't mind. Jess wasn't a bad sort. She'd come round, given time.

She hardly saw Neil Noble. He didn't seem to go out much any more. By the time term started it didn't matter anyway because he was up at the secondary school on the other side of town. Frank had no reason to be afraid in the playground and began to enjoy herself.

She stuck up for Nick, got teased by some kids for hanging around with him, but that was to be expected. A lot of them had grown up during the holidays and there seemed less will in the air to be mean to him. School was OK, occasionally even fun.

She laughed. Was happy, mostly.

She never heard the music again.

Sometimes though, she thought she caught an echo of it, faint and barely there, in music on the radio, and sometimes something like it peeked out of someone's voice, but these times were few and far between.

And although she couldn't remember exactly how it had gone, couldn't hum it, she never forgot it. It wasn't that whenever she was sad (because sometimes things *were* still sad or frustrating or upsetting) she could take the memory of the music out and put it to her ear like a shell and become happy again. It wasn't that, but it was *a little* like that.

Nowadays she was happy to wake up in the morning. That was enough.

That autumn she tried to learn the recorder again.

She gave it up before Bonfire Night.

A week before they broke up for the Christmas holidays, in one of the last sunny and surprisingly warm days of the year, she was walking home across the park, past the playground, when she saw Roy and Rob over by the swings. It looked like they were playing catch. They were throwing something back and forth between them. And then she saw a kid called Peanut kneeling on the floor.

She wasn't sure of his real name. He was in Year Four, two years below her.

It looked like they had his pencil case.

As she watched, she saw Rob throw it at Roy and Roy catch it and pretend to fumble it. It flew out of his hands into the brambles that had grown up where the nettles had been back in the summer.

They laughed like great fat idiots and, knocking him to the ground as they went past, strode off out of the rec.

'Don't do this,' her stomach said. 'No need to get involved.'

'Oi!' she shouted.

Rob and Roy turned at the noise and, seeing it was her, went quiet, but they didn't stop walking.

As they left she went over to the crying kid.

'You all right?' she asked.

He wiped a snotty nose on his sleeve and said, 'Yeah.'

'Do you know what?' she said.

He looked up at her with big, wet, red eyes.

'Them two are the biggest idiots I've ever met. They're daft as donkeys.'

She held a hand out and pulled the little kid to his feet. He almost smiled.

'OK,' her stomach said. 'Good deed all done. Let's go have tea.'

But Frank, without thinking too hard about it, waded out into the brambles, her school skirt flapping round her knees, the thorns tearing through her thick tights, snagging and pricking her.

She bent down and lifted his pencil case up.

'Here you go,' she said, chucking it into his waiting hands.

He caught it, fumbled it, dropped it.

She looked down at her ragged legs.

Tiny beads of blood were dripping on to her shoes.

'Oi, Peanut,' she said. 'You got a hanky or something?'

The kid pulled a snotty piece of once-white cloth from his pocket.

'H-h-here you go,' he said.

Frank looked at his hand, small and pale and wobbling. Smiled at how simple it looked in the clear afternoon light. Just a little boy's hand. Just a square of cotton fluttering.

'Don't worry,' she said. 'You keep it. I'll clean up when I get home.'

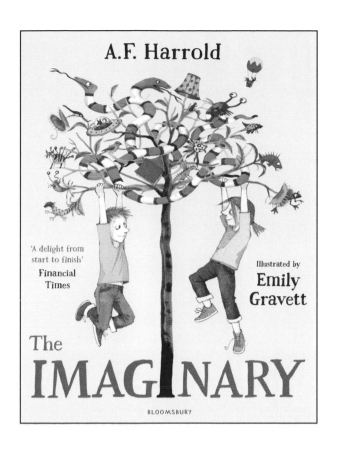

A.F. Harrold

'A delight from start to finish'
Financial Times

Illustrated by
Emily Gravett

The
IMAGINARY

BLOOMSBURY

RUDGER IS AMANDA'S BEST FRIEND.

HE DOESN'T EXIST.

BUT NOBODY'S PERFECT.

Winner of the UKLA 2016 Book Award in the 7–11 category

Longlisted for the CILIP Carnegie Medal
and the Kate Greenaway Medal 2016

Praise for *The Imaginary*

'By turns scary and funny, touching without being sentimental, and beautifully illustrated by Emily Gravett, *The Imaginary* is a delight from start to finish'

Financial Times

'A moving read about loyalty and belief in the extraordinary'

Guardian

'The kind of children's book that's the reason why adults should never stop reading children's books. Touching, exciting and wonderful to look at (Emily Gravett's illustrations are incredible), I absolutely adored this. And I cried a little bit'

Robin Stevens

'A glorious delight ... Loved it!'

Jeremy Strong

'Packed full of heart'

Phil Earle, *Guardian*

'This is young fiction of the very best quality, showcasing inspiration, inventiveness and an intoxicating passion for storytelling. *The Imaginary* has the potential to be a family favourite and a future classic'

Booktrust

'A richly visualised story which explores imaginary friends and the very special role they play in children's lives. Emily Gravett's illustrations capture the hazy world of the imaginaries brilliantly'

Julia Eccleshare, *Love Reading For Kids*